THE LAST DAYS OF

JAMES SCYTHE

report for the Ombudsman of the Pretanatural

by Lilly Banning

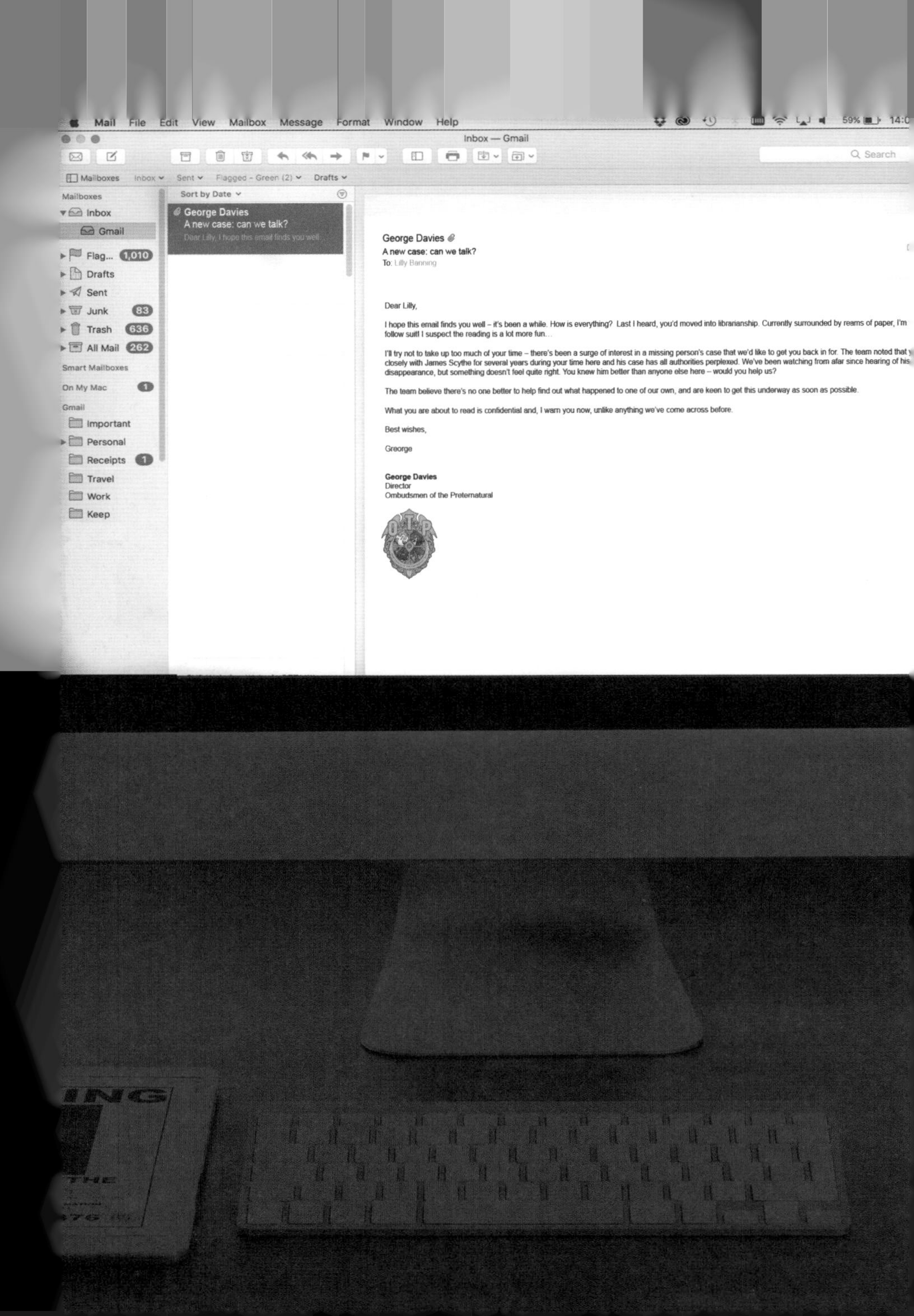

George Davies
A new case: can we talk?
To: Lilly Banning

Dear Lilly,

I hope this email finds you well – it's been a while. How is everything? Last I heard, you'd moved into librarianship. Currently surrounded by reams of paper, I'm
follow suit! I suspect the reading is a lot more fun…

I'll try not to take up too much of your time – there's been a surge of interest in a missing person's case that we'd like to get you back in for. The team noted that
closely with James Scythe for several years during your time here and his case has all authorities perplexed. We've been watching from afar since hearing of his
disappearance, but something doesn't feel quite right. You knew him better than anyone else here – would you help us?

The team believe there's no one better to help find out what happened to one of our own, and are keen to get this underway as soon as possible.

What you are about to read is confidential and, I warn you now, unlike anything we've come across before.

Best wishes,

Grerorge

George Davies
Director
Ombudsmen of the Preternatural

Writers: Will Gould, Ian Miles & David Ransom
Cover & illustration: David Ransom
Layout & design: Laura Jones
Editor: Heather McDaid
Photography (crime scene): Jay Wennington
Additional content: Leander Gloversmith

Published by 404 Ink.
404ink.com
@404Ink

ISBN: 978-0-9956238-8-0

Printed by Bell & Bain.

George Davies
A new case: can we talk?
To: Lilly Banning

13:44
Details
GD

Dear Lilly,

I hope this email finds you well – it's been a while. How is everything? Last I heard, you'd moved into librarianship. Currently surrounded by reams of paper, I'm tempted to follow suit! I suspect the reading is a lot more fun…

I'll try not to take up too much of your time – there's been a surge of interest in a missing person's case that we'd like to get you back in for. The team noted that you worked closely with James Scythe for several years during your time here and his case has all authorities perplexed. We've been watching from afar since hearing of his disappearance, but something doesn't feel quite right. You knew him better than anyone else here – would you help us?

The team believe there's no one better to help find out what happened to one of our own, and are keen to get this underway as soon as possible.

What you are about to read is confidential and, I warn you now, unlike anything we've come across before.

Best wishes,

Greorge

George Davies
Director
Ombudsmen of the Preternatural

Helvetica 12

To: George Davies

Cc:

Bcc:

Subject: Re: A new case: can we talk?

Hi George,

The James Scythe
Case Files

Notes

George Davies
A new case: can we talk?
To: Lilly Banning

13:44

Dear Lilly,

For the transparency of my investigation into the disappearance of my former colleague James Scythe, I am submitting a copy of my email correspondence with George Davies that saw me return to the team, and our initial cursory meeting.

Subject: Re: A new case: can we talk?

Hi George,

Of course – you can trust this will all be confidential. Unsurprisingly a delight to have a job surrounded by books and not having to deal with the hustle and bustle of airports and train stations all the time. It's not all timeless tales and adventures, as much as I wish it was.

I'll spare the ramblings. I had heard that James was missing and noticed there had been few updates. I had assumed (perhaps hoped) that the quietness had been that he'd been found and had just continued with his life elsewhere. Such a shame – it seems like he could never catch a break.

We owe it to James to find out what's happened. You can count me in. I'll talk to work about perhaps needing more flexible hours and make sure they know it's important without going into any details. Let's say tomorrow at 9.30am?

Best wishes,

Lilly

George Davies
Re: A new case: can we talk?
To: Lilly Banning

13:44
Details

Lilly – appreciate this. I understand the scale of what we're asking of you. I'm not sure anyone can be certain what we're working with, but I appreciate your speediness. See you tomorrow at 9.30.

George on the go
Director, OTP
Sent from iPhone

DATE: 21.03.2017
PRESENT:
STAFF: George Davies, Louise Robbins, Matthew Blake
EXTERNAL: Lilly Banning
NOTES: Craig Sharp

GD: I wanted to start by saying thank you Ms Banning for making room for us in your schedule so quickly, and agreeing to return to undertake this case. While I wasn't around to work with James, many of our staff did, and as one of our own, it's our duty to find out what happened to him, where other authorities are failing. I'll defer to Louise for the basic information.

LB: I assume you're fine with me taking notes?

GD: Of course.

LR: James came to us in 2002, having moved from Scotland following his time at university. He married Mary in 1999, who tragically lost her life in a car crash in 2006. As you will know, James was fired from this department in 2008 following a number of personal upheavals in his life. He became erratic, distracted, and was closing himself up from others. Once he left the organisation, we heard very little from him. We believe he frequently stayed in hotels around the city for reasons we're unsure of.
There had been chat around the office - do not take this as more than gossip, but it is sadly relevant - that he had become obsessed with some cult-like myths. His online postings would suggest so, but the extent to which he was involved, we cannot say. You will find links to his blogs, and copies of some of the key texts he wrote in your dossier.

MB: Jeff definitely saw him there with them, following them around-

GD: Unless it's immediately relevant could you keep to the facts, please?

LR: James was last seen on 27th Decemeber 2015 outside the Dolphin Hotel. Authorities largely tried to look at his last known movements, but quickly concluded that as a grown man he had upped and started a new life. There has been a recent resurgence of interest in this case, and the police are repeating that it is a closed case. We believe, given the research that he was deeply invested in, that this simply isn't true. A man who has spent his life investigating projects in the nature of our department, who dedicated his life to his work, loses his job, embarks on his own case and simply… gives up? This isn't James.

MB: How well did you know James?

LB: I sat across from him for a few years. We were friends. I'd hang out with his wife Mary from time to time, we'd do dinner. James' role was somewhat unusual, his methods unusual – I never knew anyone who could work like he did, and I certainly couldn't do a lot of it. I never bought into that paranormal stuff to the level he did. He would live the cases he was investigating.

After Mary death, he changed. I assume it was after then anyway, it's all a blur. Her loss hit us all hard, but James... I watched him deteriorate into a state where he couldn't do his work. He was frustrated and dishevelled. He was talking about things that, even by his standards, were... I don't know. It was a very dark time. He wasn't the same James I'd known. I was sad to see him go, but he was changing. I tried to keep in touch but he drifted away. What do you think happened to him?

MB: It seems like he-

LR: We're not here to speculate. If we knew that, we wouldn't be here.

GD: Speculation does no one any good, especially James. Let's keep this brief and focus on the files, as that's the only place where the truth will be found. We don't have many theories other than his disappearance isn't a clean slate. From his files, it feels like he was doing too much here to just cut his ties, but we're all at a loss. His motivations are hard to judge.

Even then, he's one of us, and this case can't be left to die, public scrutiny or not. That's why we need you: take as long as you need, but tell us what happened to James Scythe.

LB: You have my word that I'll do everything I can to answer that. Can I see the files?

GD: Of course. Louise, please take Ms Banning and get her the clearances she needs.

<END BRIEFING>

James Scythe

OMBUDSMEN OF THE PRETERNATURAL

ACCESS CLEARANCE

RELEASE IN PART
30B 9C

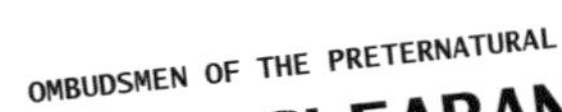

I, Lilly Banning (Please Type or Print) accept full and complete clearance of the highest level access of Ombudsmen of the Preternatural for the following case(s):

1a. The unsolved disappearance of Ombudsmen of the Preternatural employee James Sycthe

ONLY

I agree that I will access documents/audio/video recordings/archives in relation to the above case only and not request documents that are not in direct relevance to the agreed case.

I agree that I will not release any documents/audio/video recordings/archives to the general public or share the nature of their contents with anyone without explicit clearance from the Ombudsmen of the Preternatural e.g. in the example of this document, 30B9C.

REVIEW AUTHORITY: George Davies, Senior Reviewer

I agree that I will not release any documents/audio/video recordings/archives to the general public or share the nature of their contents via any methods including

a. Printing/scanning/reproduction/photographing
b. Sharing on the Internet via webpage, social media post
c. Sharing with an unauthorised party via email, post or any other methods
d. Any method not covered in this agreement that results in unauthorised parties accessing restricted information.

I agree that in the event of a discovery that breaches UK law as recognised by UK governing law following from engagement/use/deciphering of documents owned by the Ombudsmen of the Preternatural I will

a. Immediately consult the Senior Reviewer and Ombudsmen of the Preternatural Director

b. Not go directly to any Police constabularies within or outwith the UK without consulting the Senior Reviewer and the Ombudsmen of the Preternatural Director

I agree that in the event of sharing any documents accessed at any level of clearance from the Ombudsmen of the Preternatural, this agreement will be terminated and all clearance rights revoked immediately without the option of appeal. The Ombudsmen of the Preternatural are within their rights to pass any incrimiating actions by signing party caused by the voiding of this agreement to Police constabularies. The Ombudsmen of the Preternatural are not liable for any legal action to be taken against the body in the event of documents explicitly or implicitly leaked by the signing party.

L Banning

LILLY BANNING

SIGNED 03/08/2017

B30
B

C9
9

G.Davies

GEORGE DAVIES

SENIOR REVIEWER, OTP
SIGNED 03/08/2017

Other Names Used During This Period of Employment

EXTRACT ENTRY OF BIRTH : 17 & 18 Victoria Cap. 8

No.	(1) Name and Surname.	(2) When and Where Born.	(3) Sex.	(4) Name, Surname, and Rank or Profession of Father. Name, and Maiden Surname of Mother.
	James Scythe	1975 December Thirty first Kirriemuir	M.	Jeremy Scythe Agnes Scythe Agnes MacEwan

EXTRACTED from the REGISTER BOOK OF BIRTHS, for the TOWN of KIRRIEMUIR Third day of January Nineteen Hundred and Seventy Six

CERTIFIED COPY of an ENTRY OF MARRI Pursuant to the Marriage Act 19

Registration District Milbank

Marriage solemnized at the register office

t of Milbank in the City of London.

married	2 Name and surname	3 Age	4 Condition	5 Rank or profession	6 Residence at the time of marriage
nth y	James Scythe	23	———	Journalist	14 Moorgate EC2Y 9AE
9	Mary Darling	23	———	Artist	14 Moorgate EC2Y 9AE

the Register office

d James Scythe, Mary Darling in the presence of us, Andrew Clarke, Samantha Welsh

Certified to be a true copy of an entry in a register in my custody,

offence to falsify a certificate or to make or knowingly use a false certificate or a copy of a ing it to be accepted as genuine to the prejudice of any person, or to possess a certificate without lawful authority.

(5)

…alification of Informant, if out of the House in …Birth occurred.

When and … and Signa…

19 76

Scythe

January

At KIRK…

(Signed)

R. Th…

Ass…

(INIT'D)

…he .... COUNTY .... of ....

AlbertBo…
Asst

7

…ame and surname

Rank or…

Scythe

…r Darling

by Rev. Gordon Palmer

…lerford Superintendent Registrar

9th July 1999 Date

James Scythe

Former Civil Servant and Investigator

• University of London

Southampton, United Kingdom • 0

Send InMail

Investigator

Experience

Freelance

Oct 2014 – Present • 3 yrs
Various

Investigator for hire in the area of Southampton working around other current cases.
Previous cases have included:

Special Agent

Ombudsmen Of The Preternatural
Feb 2002 – Mar 2008 • 6 yrs 2 mos
London, United Kingdom

Role included:

Journalist and Editorial Assistant

News Daily London
Aug 1997 – Jan 2002 • 4 yrs 6 mos
London

Local and national stories, investigative journalism.

Education

University of London

[Redacted], [Redacted]
1993 – 1997

DEPARTMENT of INVESTIGATION

OTP

THIS CERTIFIES THAT THE SIGNATURE AND PHOTOGRAPH HEREON IS AN APPOINTED

SPECIAL AGENT: James Scythe

OMBUDSMEN OF THE PRETERNATURAL

One of two missing posters found around the city. One featured James' official work photo, and the other featured this illustration, believed to be a more accurate representation of James at the time of his disappearance. We've been unable to locate who put these posters up, and while at a glance we believed it could have been tied to the Hampshire Constabulary, the number appears to be a hoax noting that callers will "die holding hands" on October 2nd.

MISSI
Last seen
Dolphin Hotel
JAMES SCYT
MISSING SINCE: 27/12/2015
LAST SEEN: SOUTHAMPTON, UK
D.O.B: 31/12/1975
BLACK HAIR, GREEN EYES, 6ft 1in, 77 kg /
PERSONS HAVING ANY INFORMATIO
ARE REQUESTED TO CALL
HAMPSHIRE CONSTABULARY
023-8000-0376

CAM 1
Last spotted on CCTV early hours of 27th December

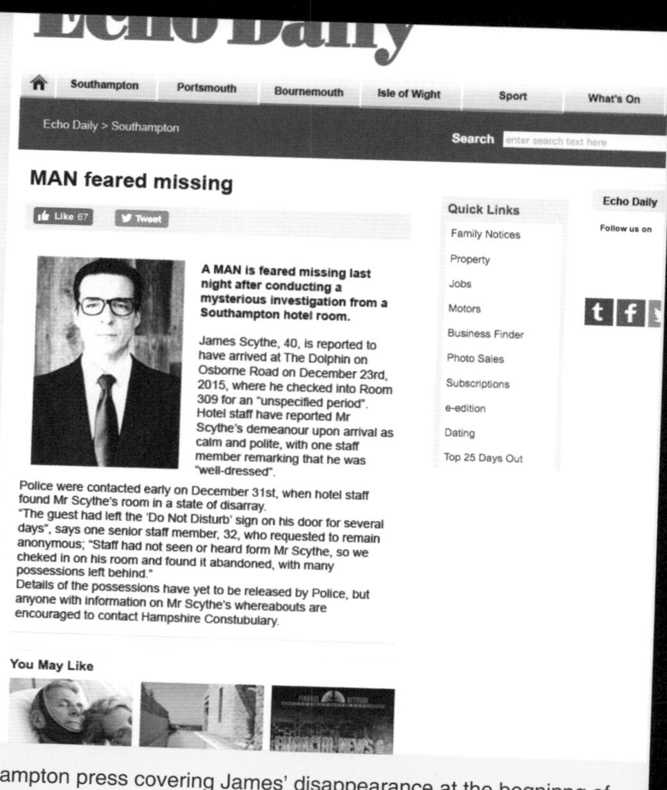

Echo Daily

Southampton | Portsmouth | Bournemouth | Isle of Wight | Sport | What's On

Echo Daily > Southampton

Search

MAN feared missing

Like 67 Tweet

A MAN is feared missing last night after conducting a mysterious investigation from a Southampton hotel room.

James Scythe, 40, is reported to have arrived at The Dolphin on Osborne Road on December 23rd, 2015, where he checked into Room 309 for an "unspecified period". Hotel staff have reported Mr Scythe's demeanour upon arrival as calm and polite, with one staff member remarking that he was "well-dressed".

Police were contacted early on December 31st, when hotel staff found Mr Scythe's room in a state of disarray.

"The guest had left the 'Do Not Disturb' sign on his door for several days", says one senior staff member, 32, who requested to remain anonymous; "Staff had not seen or heard form Mr Scythe, so we cheked in on his room and found it abandoned, with many possessions left behind."

Details of the possessions have yet to be released by Police, but anyone with information on Mr Scythe's whereabouts are encouraged to contact Hampshire Constubulary.

You May Like

Quick Links

- Family Notices
- Property
- Jobs
- Motors
- Business Finder
- Photo Sales
- Subscriptions
- e-edition
- Dating
- Top 25 Days Out

Echo Daily

Follow us on

Local Southampton press covering James' disappearance at the beginning of January 2016.
Was potentially lost over Christmas?
Not much engagement on article.

FATAL FRIDAY

THE CRASH IS BEING TREATED AS AN ACCIDENT, HOWEVER THE HAMPSHIRE POLICE, WHEN REACHED FOR COMMENT, RELEASED THE FOLLOWING STATEMENT: "THERE HAS BEEN ONE FATALITY, AND ONE SURVIVOR CURRENTLY IN HOSPITAL, WHO WAS THE DRIVER OF THE VEHICLE. WE ARE NOT AT LIBERTY TO DISCUSS THIS FURTHER, THOUGH OUR THOUGHTS GO OUT TO THE FAMILIES OF THOSE INVOLVED. THERE WILL BE AN UPDATE WHEN ROADS WILL REOPEN FULLY."

A WITNESS, WHO ASKED TO REMAIN ANONYMOUS, CONTACTED THE PAPER AND CLAIMED THAT MR. SCYTHE COULD BE HEARD REPEATEDLY MENTIONING "A DARK CLOAKED FIGURE" WHILE BEING TAKEN INTO HOSPITAL IN THE EARLY HOURS OF THE MORNING AND WAS BECOMING IRATE WHEN STAFF DIDN'T APPEAR TO BE LISTENING TO HIS CONCERNS. "I WOULD FEEL BAD IF THERE WAS SOMEONE ON THE ROAD THAT CAUSED THE CRASH AND PEOPLE WEREN'T LISTENING, BUT REALLY – IT'S PROBABLY JUST SHOCK. MIGHT HAVE THOUGHT IT WAS THE GRIM REAPER OR SOMETHING." WE HAVE BEEN ABLE TO VERIFY THEIR LOCATION, AND HAVE ALERTED AUTHORITIES OF THIS CLAIM.

SECTIONS OF THE M27 ARE DUE TO CONTINUE RUNNING AS A SINGLE LANE UNTIL AT LEAST 5PM TODAY. COMMUTERS ARE URGED TO FIND ALTERNATIVE ROUTES TO AVOID DELAYS.

FATAL FRIDAY

MARY

A WOMAN was killed last night after a vehicle swerved from the motorway.

Police have cordoned off a section of the M27 this morning causing Saturday shopper traffic chaos, after a car hit a stretch of black ice at 11PM on Friday night.

Passenger Mary Scythe, 30, suffered fatal injuries on December 23rd when the vehicle was thrown from the road, crashed through motorway barriers and collided with a tree at high speed.

Her husband, James Scythe, 31, was driving at the time of the collision and has survived but sustained severe injuries to his left hand.

Paramedic reports from the scene confirmed that Mr Scythe was airlifted to Southampton Hospital in *"a state of extreme shock."* Continues Page 5

TRAGIC: *Crash horro*

1
1
MUFON
ELVIS
by Jerry Hopkins
5
3
9
2
ESP
???

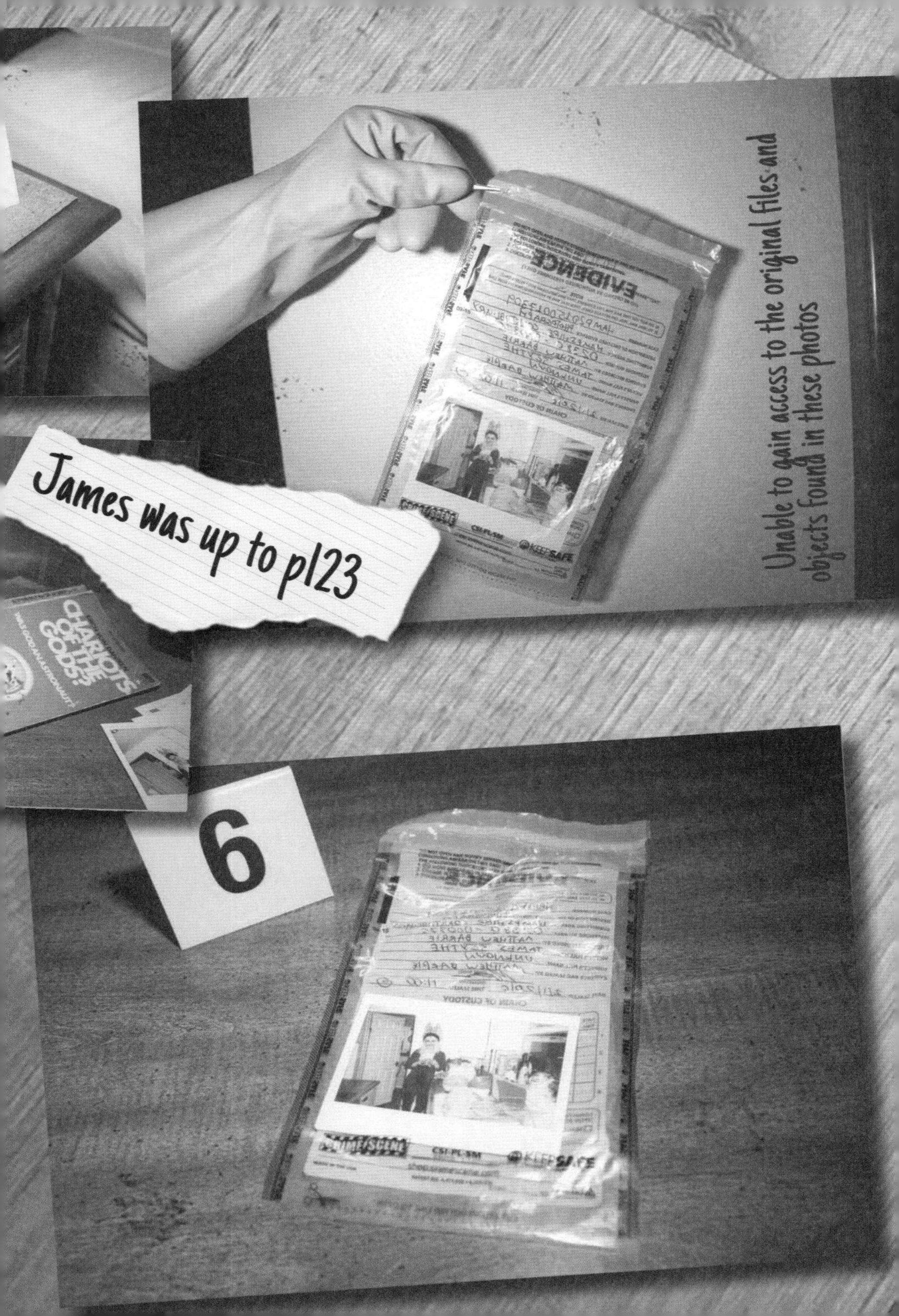
James was up to pl23
Unable to gain access to the original files and objects found in these photos
CHARIOTS OF THE GODS?
EVIDENCE
CHAIN OF CUSTODY
CSI·PL·SM
KEEPSAFE
6

Ombudsman of the Preternatural badge –
he was meant to turn this in when he left
OTP
8
10
Fortean Times
SCOTLAND YARD'S SECRETS
HEX AND VIOLENCE
THE CURIOUS CASE OF THE HEADLESS EVANGELIST
MODERN ART IS MURDER
A WOOLF IN THE FOLD
History of the World
OCCULT SCIENCE
MAN'S HEAD SEVERED
BY NEIGHBOR
Fortean Times
DARKNESS VISIBLE
THE GHOST OF BERKELEY SQUARE
LONDON

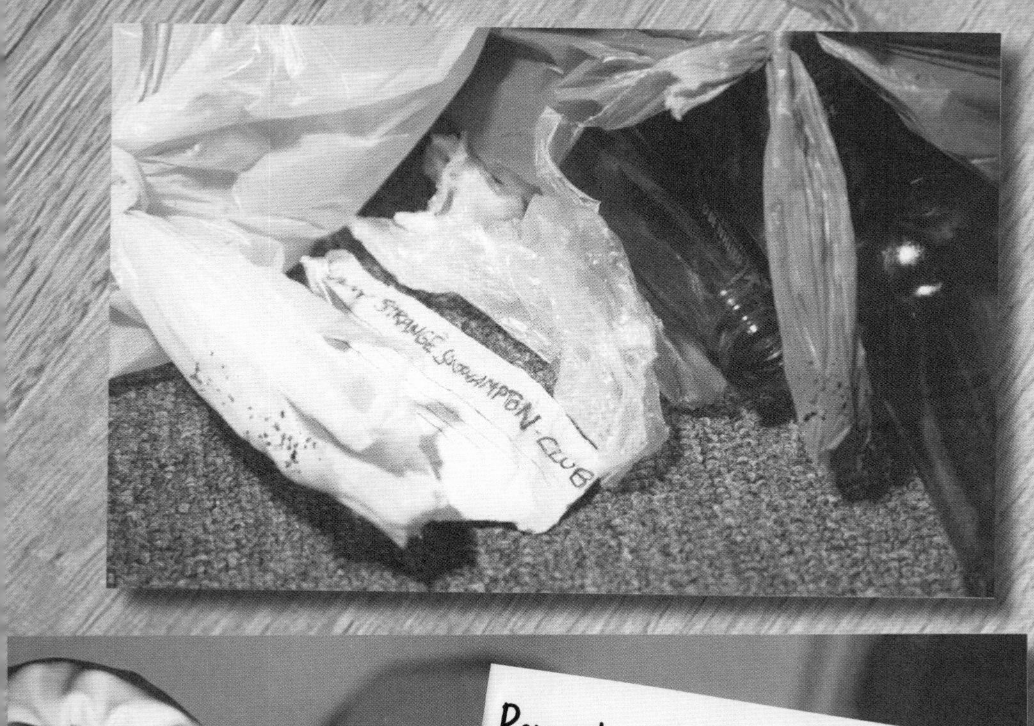

Remember, check this website

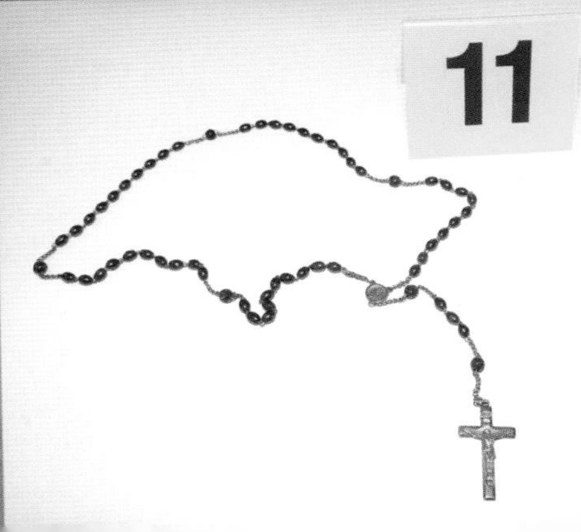

Spoke to a number of people who had either known, met or encountered James in some capacity and typed up some notes on my old typewriter while my laptop is on the blink

Included:

- My own notes as a former colleague
- Matthew Blake. former colleague
- Floyd Gibbs, former landlord in London
- Terry Harding, regular at the Ticking Ship pub
- Laura Cruz, receptionist at The Dolphin hotel
- Julia Tate, jogger in Southampton
- Alexis Holt, staff member at local supermarket
- Nathan Hodges, barman at the Ticking Ship

In our last weeks prior to Jame[...] become erratic through grief. He hadn't cop[...] wife and came back to work far too soon. He was adam[...] was work to be done on cases no one else had note of. James ha[...] worked in the fringes of our job, the cases that I wouldn't take on. I [...] lieve in the unordinary, but James believed in almost otherworldly ideas. His desk became piles of paper that he'd let topple onto the fl[...] and leave there, he'd get irate if anyone touched his desk. He cut hi[...] self off from most of the staff – he'd still talk to me occasionally but was quieter. He felt frantic. When our former manager arranged fo[...] desk to be sorted James was beside himself, flew into a fit of rage a[...] weeks of near silence from him and was let go of the next day. I tr[...] stay in touch with him but he got rid of most of his socials, chang[...] number. I assumed he'd moved away and got a fresh start, may[...] easier to think that way than keep worrying. He wasn't the sa[...] the accident.

...obably not the best way to go about
...was said around the office. Look, I'm sorry. I
...ard time, but you asked—

...eally know James. He came to me saying he'd just sold his home that he'd
...with his wife and was in need of a flat, seemed nice enough, paid promptly
...ever had any issues. We never spoke until he handed in his
...ound October 2009 after his first six months was up
...he had to leave. Not sure where he went.
...nt I ever had.

I heard you were askin...
world at large over a pint. Rea...
why we became friends! What did we talk about? This and that, just whatever ...h, suppose that's
was on the news that day, sports – he really hated cricket. Yeah, it's such a
...hame what happened to James Smythe [sic], I really hope you are able to find
...im or at least find peace for his story.

...end of t...
Of course, tow...
2015 I mean. He'd c...
every morning for breakfa...
almost always wearing a suit.
Smile, say hello, keep himself to
himself. He'd ask if he could have
the papers from the previous day to
spare them getting thrown out. Never
really asked what he was doing, not really
our business, is it? One morning in
December he didn't come down for
breakfast and his room had the 'do not
disturb' sign so cleaners skipped it, but just
assumed he was unwell. Couldn't tell you th...
exact date. Day four or five the staff were
concerned he'd maybe fallen, so checked
and he was gone. It's a shame he's still
not been found.

I saw your call out for information on James Scythe and wanted to get in touch. I know it's probably nothing, but he used to come in here every now and then and get papers. Really liked the Echo Daily, said the hotel he was in didn't always have that on hand. Also picked up some of our quirky UFOlogy mags on occasion for his kid to keep his kids imagination alive. Cute I thought. I checked the CCTV and the last day he came in here was December 15th. Just got a packet of cigs and some juice. Ordinary day.

I only know what was said around the office. James was one of the best there was, the accident happened, he lost his way a little. I didn't work near him, just saw him around carrying notebooks and coffee everywhere. I remember when I first started he was like the guy, you know? Crisp, slick, funny, you just wanted to be his friend. He was a bit messy by the end, had a beard – there's nothing wrong with beards though! It just seemed the latest thing in him not taking care of himself.

People joked he was getting into forums online, proper tinfoil hat stuff, even for us. Few of them saw him wandering at night about ten yards away from groups of folk, trying to take them back to his home planet. Or trying to become part of the cool gang. Anyway, he was a proper lurker. Never did anything, just seemed to walk around following people who were having a more fun life than he was. Probably trying to relive his youth, or get laid. Probably not the best way to go about it. Yeah, I know. I said I only know what was said around the office. Look, I'm sorry. I know he was having a hard time, but you asked—

Pretty sure we jogged the same route from time to time. Didn't chat much on the times we jogged together but he was really built. Deceptively so. He had a number of tattoos I was in awe of – the Mrs won't let me get any. Umm, the last time would be New Year's Eve – he wasn't excited about Christmas or New Years, wanted the in-la using the jog as a way to avoid getting ready for Christmas dinner.

ames? He was here quite a lot. Same drink every time – gle malt, neat. He'd not mind which one. He was nice enough. Quite Never caused any trouble. He'd carry a little brown notebook with him – he was an artist and kept it in case inspiration took him. Asked him once if I d see his artwork and he got quite defensive, so I never asked again. Stopped hristmas – figured the season wasn't his thing. A lot of people ck of Christmas tunes and tinsel when it's been on for so many weeks already.

J. S TIMELINE

1993	Meets Mary
1993-1997	University
1997-2002	Editorial assistant and journalist at The News Daily London
February 2002	Begins work at OTP / work at OTP
2006	Wife Mary dies in car wreck / descent from PTSD
March 2008 (33yrs old)	Fired from OTP /spiral out of control
2009	Sold his home - Milbank - moved into old family home
March 2009	Moved into flat - Camden
October 2009	Moved out of flat
2009-2014	?
2014 / 2015	Arrives in Southampton
15th December 2015	Last seen at shop
Mid-December 2015	Last seen at bar
20-something December 2015	Stopped coming for breakfast at hotel / room found empty
31 December 2015	Reportedly jogging

???

TIME OUT PHASE
why only here?
LACK MASS
THE SOUTHAMPTON
Shirley
Freemantle
Banister Park
Fitzhugh
The Polygon
Bevois Town
Westwood Park
King Edward VI School
Southampton Old Cemetery
British American Tobacco
Millbrook (Hants)
Vehicle Holding Compound
Southampton Central
South Western Main Line
Millbrook Road West
Millbrook Road East
Mountbatten Way
West Bay Road
Herbert Walker Avenue
West Quay Road
Hill Lane
Shirley Road
Howard Road
Archers Road
Raymond Road
Waterloo Road
Paynes Road
Western Avenue
Berth 109
Berth 108
Berth 104
Berth 103
Berth 102
Berth 101
Berth SCT 5
Upper Swinging Ground
Middle Swinging Ground
Lower Swinging Ground
Marchwood Basin
Marchwood Channel
Marchwood Wharf
Marchwood Power Station
Husbands Ship Yard
Mulberry Wharf
Falkland Wharf
Gunwharf
McMullen Barracks
Marchwood Military Port
Royal Pier (ruins)
Red Funnel Terminal 2 (Red Jet)
Berth 50
Berth 49
Berth 48
Castle Way
High Street
East Street
A33
A3057
A3024
A35
Test

00:00:03:04
Down Below
3rd Sighting
St Denys
North Road
South Road
Adelaide Road
Ivy Road
Priory Road
Belmont Road
Osborne Road South
Westridge Road
A3035
Thorold Road
Cobden Avenue
Whitworth Crescent
Whitworth Road
Macnaghten Road
Cobbett Road
Midanbury Lane
Nesa Road
St Mary's College
Beech Avenue
Vale Drive
High View Way
Vanguard Road
Mousehole Lane
Lytham Road
Exeter Road
Townhill Way
Gorselands Road
West End Road
Yeovil Chase
Somerton Avenue
Wellington Avenue
Taunton Drive
Balaclava Road
Marne Road
Shales Road
Dean Road
Pound Street
West End Road
Wavell Road
Rossington Avenue
Glenfield Avenue
Glenfield Crescent
Chafen Road
A3024
Bitterne
Steuart Road
Quayside Road
Maybray King Way
York Drove
Bitterne Road
A334
Keats Road
Chessel Crescent
Chessel Avenue
Little Lances Hill
Angel Crescent
Bitterne Way
Athelstan Road
Bath Road
Brownlow Avenue
Downside Avenue
Freemantle Common
Driver's Wharf
(ruins)
Princes Street
Millstone Point
Northam
Bond Street
William Street
Millbank Street
Shamrock Quay
Bakers Wharf
James Wharf
Dibles wharf
Britannia Road
Itchen
West Coastway Line
Braeside Road
Peartree Avenue
Chatsworth Road
Ruby Road
White's Road
Spring Road
Magnolia Road
Acacia Road
Deacon Road
Saint Aubin's Avenue
Bursledon Road
Barry Road
Upper Deacon
Lime Avenue
Firtree Way
North East Road
High Firs Road
Blackthorn Road
Merryoak Road
Merridale Road
Gainsford Road
Bryanston Road
Heath Road
Sholing Road
Sholing
Kathleen Road
Banbury
Britannia Wharf
Burnley Wharf
Peartree Green
American Wharf
Hazel Road
Peartree Road
Mortimer Road
Ludlow Road
Bishops Road
Pooley Road
Pinegrove Road
Loane Road
South East Road
Kathleen Road
Chadwell Avenue
Alfriston Gardens
Julian Road
Butt's Road
Millais Road
Leighton Road
Knighton Road
Radstock Road
St Monica Road
Bay Road
Botany Bay Road
Itchen Bridge
A3025
Woolston Railway Station
Porchester Road
Portsmouth Road
Station Road
Heathfield Road
Ashby Road
Inkerman Road
Florence Road
Obelisk Road
West Road
Canada Road
St Anne's Road
Sholing Railway Station
St Mary Extra Cemetery
Wright's Hill
Botley Road
Woolston Riverside Centenary Quay
Berth 29
Church Road
College Road
Swift Road
Archery Grove
Weston Lane
Newtown Road
Cox's Drive
The Grove
Victoria Road
Glen Road
Mayfield Park
Newtown
Berth 30
Weston Allotments
Jurds Lake Way
Archery Road
Scott Road
Weston Point
Chamberlayne College for the Arts
Weston Lane
Wallace Road
Tickleford Drive
Kingsclere Avenue
Weston
Ropley Close
Weston Shelf
Moorings
Pitch & Putt
Weston Parade
Woolston Road
Grange Road
Cranmore
East Mud

JS

"Trust ye not in a friend,
put ye not confidence
in a guide."

OCTOBER 2014

THE PAGES WITHIN CONSIDER A WORLD IN WHICH
I HAVE FOUND MYSELF FALLING INTO, AND
NEED TO DOCUMENT SO THE WORLD KNOWS.

THOUGH, IF YOU'RE READING THIS, GOD ONLY
KNOWS WHAT'S HAPPENED TO ME. IF THIS IS IN
YOUR HANDS, DO WHAT YOU HAVE TO DO TO
MAKE EVERYONE UNDERSTAND.
I HOPE IT NEVER COMES TO THAT.

J. SCYTHE

Hello.

Hello world. I can't say this will be the most interesting of introductions to read, but WordPress tells me to say hello to the world, so here I am.

I'm finding my wasted minutes blurring into hours reading others' blogs of investigations and subjects that people often don't dig deep enough into. I've spent my life following such mysteries, so why change now? I'd like to think that down the line I might be able to join the ranks of those I'm falling in wormholes into – wouldn't it be great for Strange Southampton to not have to do all their brilliant work solo? – but time will tell if I uncover what I'm after.

Follow me if you'd like

J

❑ jamesscythe ❑

❑ 1 Min

Spectral J

PROPE
OF O

≡ Menu

Ep. 20 recap, part 1.

Hello all,

Working backwards as promised. Episode 20 combines two legends in one, the reason for v because they are both centred around Southampton, a place in which I've actually been in la won't repeat too many details on Southampton as we discussed that alongside Belfast in our on the Titanic, but there's some mysterious stuff lurking beneath the surface in the city.

Part 1 will focus on the background information from the podcast. I don't want to leave it too get on with writing these up, but I'm currently looking into the phenomena discussed in the e so may be able to add more detail and thought this would be a good place to start.

Background:

Southampton is home to the Medieval Merchants House, one of the earliest surviving houses in England (13th century). During WWII it was seemingly a brothel. Visitors often see doors slam, feel ghostly presences tap them on the shoulder when visiting.

The Tudor House also goes back to the 1400s. The police are frequently called to investigate brea overheard only to discover no signs of a break in, but all the lights turned on. This happened so c a medium was called in to assist the restless spirits; I can't find a report on whether she was successful or not.

There's a high number of UFO sightings here – in 2009 the Government declassified over 800 UFO files, a high volume of which were based in Southampton, causing local press interest in the topic f the first time in many years. It marked a nice return to the topic given the city's history with one of the longest running UFO groups within all British UFOlogy – SUFOG. Southampton UFO Group. It ran since 1990.

For more on taking a ghost walk and visiting these old homes, visit hauntedsouthampton.com

If you would like to research more on the city's UFO history, visit http://www.sufog.freeserve.co.uk (http://www.sufog.freeserve.co.uk).

Do look into the websites for more background information while I continue with the writing. These are some of the most enthralling cases to look into and I hope you find as much interest as I do. When you're dealing with an almost timeless mystery rather than the past, there's always more informa unfurling around you.

Until next time.

J

spectraljames.wordpress.com

- First blog in September 2014
- Strange Southampton – remember seeing this when glancing through files. Mentioned as a potential peer / inspiration to his blog. "Brilliant work" – look into
- Ran podcast – Spectral Sceptic. Looked into mysteries – think Jack the Ripper, Area 51.
— Reportedly sound files glitched, asked listeners to stockpile files for him as back up. I had a look and it seems someone has reuploaded them to a new Soundcloud as he asked, but since James' disappearance. 95% are glitched, only one in full is on The Callous Heart and The Stranger
— Appears to be the final podcast – Spectral Sceptic stopped after, or files unrecovered
— Have included a screenshot of this blog in the core files, the most comprehensive available. Likely to show where his focus was
— How nice to hear him after all this time – he doesn't exactly sound happy, but sounds more his business-like, focused self. More the James we knew
- Last blog posted 9th December 2015, ended with:

"I feel this investigation coming to a head. I'm not sure how much longer the blog will continue, but emails are always open. Don't be a stranger."

PROPERTY OF OTP

STRANGE SOUTHAMPTON

STRANGESOUTHAMPTON.CLUB

WHO RUNS THIS?? NOT HEARD BACK VIA EMAIL BUT NEED TO FIND THEM.

KEY NOTES ON SOUTHAMPTON:

REALMS OF SUPER AND PRETERNATURAL, FELT MYSTIC ENERGIES CONVERGE IN AND AROUND SOUTHAMPTON. TITANIC SET OFF FROM A CITY THAT IS A HOTBED FOR DARK SPIRITS AND INEXPLICABLE SIGHTINGS AND GOINGS ON! DON'T LET THE QUAINT TOURIST TRAILS FOOL YOU — SOUTHAMPTON'S AWASH WITH HAUNTED PLACES; ITS HISTORY IS STEEPED IN TALES OF MISERY AND LOSS, AND TORMENTED SPIRITS OLD AND ETERNALLY YOUNG STALK THESE STREETS PAVED WITH GRIEF.

COMFORT TO HIM?

????

OTHER SECTIONS: GHOST WALK, TUDOR HOUSE, MERCHANTS HALL, SOUTH WESTERN HOTEL, UFOS OVER SOUTHAMPTON CITY CENTRE. NO REFERENCE TO THESE IN JAMES' NOTES. KEEP IN MIND IF THEY APPEAR.

Strange
Southampton
FACEBOOK.COM/STRANGESOUTHAMPTON
"make yourselves (un)comfortable."
2/2/17

FOUND WEGDED IN J'S NOTEBOOK

LOCATIONS EXPLORED!

...TERIES ...OVERED!

...familiar with the haunting tale of 'The ... legends. But, are the stories of the hooded ...ss o'er her bed" just folklore, or a terrifying

...ou on a nail-biting journey into the dark ...pots of mystical convergence, where ...n reported, ever since the torrid day of

...y of this masked fiend's reign of fear, ... ghost story, tracing its sinister ...nt day.

...ger himself, lurking in the cursed

"And he'll come to see you,
In the window of your home. . ."

BOOK NOW for your place on this nail-biting exploration of Southampton's most sinister secret: "The Stranger."

Brought to you by Titanic Tours™ Ltd., the 'Stranger Walk' is the only way to get up close and uncomfortable with the city's most enduring haunting.

ADULT: Tour may contain jump scares and mild peril. Not recommended for children under the age of 14. Under 16s must be accompanied by an adult. Parental discretion is advised.

WE ARE HERE!

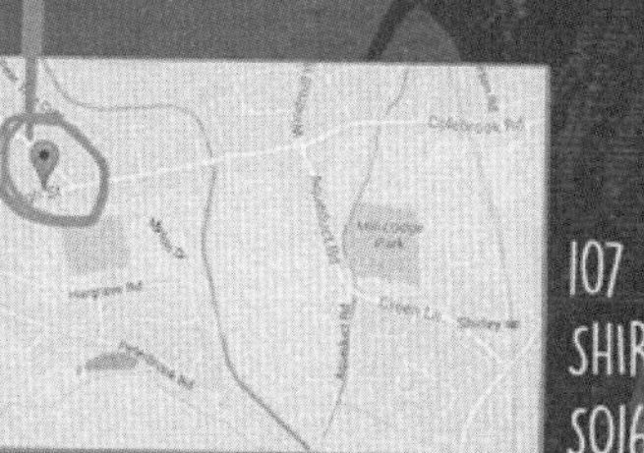

107 HIGH ST.
SHIRLEY
SO16 4EY

THE SOUTHAMPTON STRANGER WALK

WITNESS THE STORY OF
OUR HAUNTED MARINE CITY...

IF YOU DARE!!!

BOOK NOW!
023 8000 0376

SOUTHAMPTON UFO GROUP

NEWSLETTER

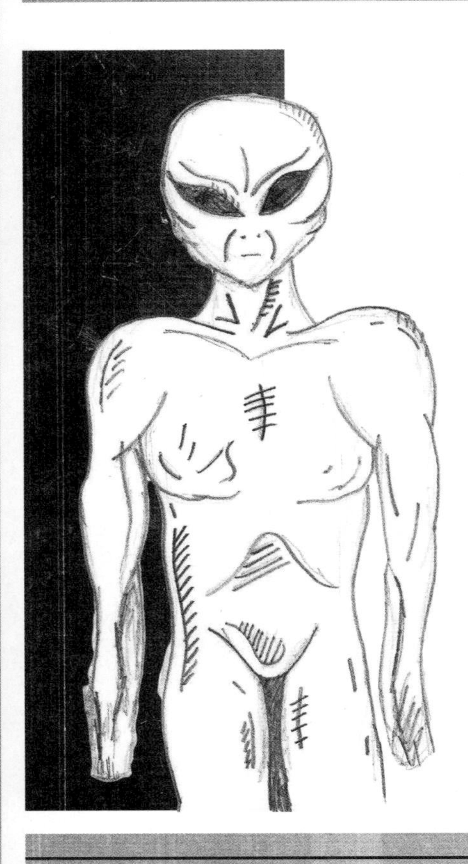

CONTENT

ORGANISER:
STEVE
GERRARD TEL:
0703 309194

25 WESTO
ROAD W
SOUT
HAMPS

PROPERTY OF OTL

D
GI
SC
AB
DIN
APP
ANI
BEF
MAN
AUT
INCI
IN AN
PINK
ESTAT
CARR
DISINT
AND T
WOOLS
THE OL
FIRSTLY
HER 13-
SAME PH
BEHAVIN
KNOWN
THEIR DE
IF ANYON
SOUTHAM
MOBILE 0
ERNIE SEA

CALL FOR UFO WITNESSES

DID YOU WITNESS A STRANGE PHENOMENON IN THE SKIES ABOVE BASINSTOKE ON MARCH 3?

THE SOUTHAMPTON FO GROUP HAS BEEN BUSY INVESTIGATING A REPORT OF AN UNIDENTIFIED FLYING OBJECT ABOUT BASINGSTOKE ON THAT NIGHT – BUT SO FAR, NO EXPLANATION HAS BEEN FOUND.

STEVE RIDER, SOUTHAMPTON UFO GROUP INVESTIGATOR, EXPLAINED: THE EYEWITNESS SAW 20 TO 30 OBJECTS ARRANGED IN TWO LINE IN A V-FORMATION. THE OBJECTS WERE "ZIG-ZAGGING" AND GLOWING ORANGE/RED.

HE SAID THE FORMATION MOVED IN AN EASTERLY DIRECTION AND WAS DESCRIBED AS SIMILAR TO THE "LUBBOCK LIGHTS" SEEN OVER TEXAS IN AMERICA IN THE 1950S.

"THAT WAS A CLASSIC CASE WHICH IS NAMED AFTER THE PLACE IN TEXAS WHERE A V-FORMATION WAS SEEN AND PHOTOGRAPHER. THERE HAVE BEEN OTHER SIGHTINGS OF V-FORMATIONS BUT THIS IS THE FIRST I HAVE HEARD OF IN THAT PARTICULAR SHAPE DOWN HER IN THE SOUTH," SAID MR RIDER.

THE GROUP HAS CONTACTED GATWICK AND HEATHROW AIRPORTS, AS WELL AS THE UFO REPORTING DESK AT THE MINISTRY OF DEFENCE.

"THEY ALL CAME UP WITH NOTHING ELSE ON THAT DATE," ADDED MR RIDER.

A SPOKESMAN FOR BASINGSTOKE POLICE TOLD THE GAZETTE HE WAS ALSO UNABLE TO SHED ANY LIGHT ON THE STRANGE SIGHTING.

MR RIDER SAID: "THE WITNESS IS A PILOT SO HE'S USED TO SEEING A LOT OF DIFFERENT THINGS IN THE SKY. BUT HE SAID HE'S NEVER SEEN ANYTHING QUITE LIKE THIS BEFORE."

HE ADDED: "AS OF THIS YEAR, THIS IS THE ONLY UFO

DLES

NING OF MAY 19 A MYSTERIOUS
GHT WAS SEEN HOVERING OVER
ATER FOR SOME TIME, MOVING
ALLY AND SHOWING, BRIEFLY A
D A STROBE. AN AIRCRAFT
HE SOUTHAMPTON DOCKS AREA
OTHER OBJECT SEVERAL TIMES
G AND THEN REPEATING THE
OUGH A VIDEO FILM SHOW THIS,
D ALL KNOWLEDGE OF THE
ING ANOTHER MYSTERY!
T ON JUNE 20 A BRILLIANT
RED OVER THE INGLESIDE
BBEY IN THE EVENING. IT ALSO
LIGHTS, ONE OF WHICH
E THE OTHER GOT BRIGHTER
RITION SPED OFF TOWARDS

THE SAME PERCIPIENT,
BAND, AND SECONDLY WITH
HAD SEEN THE APPARENTLY
BOXING NIGHT 1999,
MANNER. WITNESSES ARE
E NO DOUBT AT ALL THE

ASE CONTACT
P ON 023 8045 6000 OR

EY

UFO CLUB CALLS IT A DAY

FIRST THERE WAS THE SIGHTING OF THE MYSTERIOUS MULTI-COLOURED CHANDELIER-SHAPED OBJECT HOVERING IN THE SOUTH'S SKIES.

THEN THERE WAS THE FAST-MOVING BRIGHT LIGHT SPOTTED OVER BEAULIEU IN THE NEW FOREST.

AND THEN, A FEW YEARS LATER, THERE WERE REPORTS OF HOODED FIGURES IN THE STREETS OF SOUTHAMPTON.

THESE ARE ALL AMONG THE BIZARRE, ODD AND UNEXPLAINED SIGHTINGS OF A GROUP OF UFO SPOTTERS MONITORING THE SKIES ABOVE HAMPSHIRE.

BUT NOW, AFTER ALMOST 20 YEARS OF NO DEFINITIVE EVIDENCE AND A FEW UNANSWERED QUESTIONS, THEY HAVE DECIDED TO FOLD UP THEIR TELESCOPES.

WITH THE HELP OF SCI-FI SHOWS SUCH AS THE X-FILES, IN THE EARLY 1990S THE POPULARITY OF HUNTING FOR EXTRA-TERRESTRIALS WAS SKY-HIGH AND SOUTHAMPTON UFO GROUP (SUFOG) BOASTED MORE THAN 75 MEMBERS.

BUT SINCE THEN THERE HAS BEEN A WANE IN INTERGALACTIC INTEREST AND FOUNDING MEMBER STEVE GERRARD HAS DECIDED TO SHUT THE GROUP DOWN AFTER ONLY FOUR MEMBERS TURNED UP TO ITS LAST MEETING.

THE GROUP STARTED IN NOVEMBER 1990, WHEN STEVE PUT AN ADVERT IN THE BACK OF THE DAILY ECHO LOOKING FOR EXTRATERRESTRIAL ENTHUSIASTS.

OVER THE YEARS THEIR PHOTOS OF STRANGE OBJECTS IN THE SKY HAVE BEEN SPLASHED ACROSS THE WORLD'S MEDIA, AND THE MINISTRY OF DEFENCE HAS EVEN INVESTIGATED THEIR VIDEO FOOTAGE.

ONE OF THE ORIGINAL MEMBERS, ERNIE SEARS, SAID THE GROUP HAS TAKEN HUNDREDS OF PHOTOGRAPHS DURING THEIR SKY-WATCHES, BUT SAID THERE WAS ONE INCIDENT THAT "CHANGED HIS LIFE FOREVER".

ERNIE, 83, OF NETLEY, SAID: "I HAD MY FIRST SIGHTING IN MARCH 1960 AT PORTSDOWN HILL. I SAW A VERY STRANGE-LOOKING LIGHT IN THE SKY. I THOUGHT IT MUST BE AN AIRCRAFT WITH THE SUN REFLECTING OFF IT. BUT IT SEEMED TO BE HANGING THERE AND I THOUGHT: IT CAN'T BE ONE OF THOSE PESKY UFOS.' "HALF AN HOUR LATER I HEARD THE ROAR OF JET ENGINES. I RUSHED TO AN OPENING AND SAW TWO METEOR JETS FLYING LOW OVER GOSPORT, COMING FROM THE DIRECTION OF THORNY ISLAND AERODROME.

"TO MY AMAZEMENT THIS OBJECT WAS STILL HANGING IN THE SKY IN THE SAME PLACE AND NOT MOVING. I KNEW THEN THAT IT WASN'T AN AIRCRAFT.

"I WATCHED AS THE JETS NEARED IT BUT AS THEY DID IT TURNED ON END AND DISAPPEARED INTO THE BLUE SKY LIKE A LIGHT BEING SWITCHED OFF.

"I RAN INTO A PHONE BOX AND PHONED THORNY ISLAND AIR CONTROL. I ASKED HIM IF HE COULD TELL ME WHAT THE OBJECT WAS THE METEOR JETS WERE CHASING. I'LL NEVER FORGET HIS ANSWER. HE SAID: YOU DID NOT SEE ANY OBJECT AND YOU DID NOT SEE ANY METEOR JETS.' "SINCE THEN I HAVE BEEN CONVINCED THERE IS OTHER LIFE OUT THERE AND I AM DETERMINED TO PROVE IT'S TRUE."

TRANSCRIPT
Interview with Carl Soter, Hampshire based UFOlogist
January 19th 1999

Audio starts at [0:12:15]

Interviewer: So to begin would you mind introducing yourself and giving us a little background on your work?

Carl Soter: Absolutely. My name is Carl Soter and the majority of my work has been based upon the research of UFO phenomena across the southern coast of the UK. I've written two published papers on the subject and have been a guest speaker at numerous events around the world.

Interviewer: Excellent, thank you, Carl. The first question I'd like to ask you is when was it you found yourself drawn to the UFO topic? Have you an earliest memory of being attracted to the lights in our sky?

Carl Soter: What I actually find most common with people in our field is that that the world of UFOlogy often finds us. To answer your question, the earliest memory I have of it impacting my life is one from when I was a child, maybe nine or ten years old. It was dark out and I was driving with my father back to Southampton after a weekend away. We were passing through the New Forest when from the back seat of the car I noticed something in the sky.

It was three lights in triangle formation hovering maybe 50 feet above the ground. I was absolutely amazed. I shouted for my father but just as I had his attention, the trio of lights blinked and then shot up into the sky.

It was at a pace I'd never seen before and have never seen again.

Interviewer: What did your father have to say about all this if you don't mind me asking?

Carl Soter: This is just it; he didn't see the craft at all. By the time he had heard me, it had already zipped up into the air. I tried to explain later on to him but sadly he never believed me.

Interviewer: thus introducing you to your first of the skeptics and non-believers that come with this territory!

[Laughing]

Carl Soter: yes I guess so!

Interviewer: So tell me, how do you deal with people like this? I suppose it must be frustrating to have to fight to be taken seriously all the time.

Carl Soter: I try to be understanding. We are asking people to question everything they've been brought up to believe. The UFO phenomenon is so much bigger than an unidentified light in the sky. These things move at incredible pace and then come to a complete stop in a split second. The thing is, these phenomena aren't just reported by civilians. Every year hundreds of airforce and government personnel report these sightings too. We've gotten to a point where it is very hard to argue that these things aren't happening. So what really bugs the skeptics is the argument as to what they are. The way I see it, they are either super advanced military vehicles or just perhaps they are from another planet. Either way, someone knows what they are and refuses to share it with us.

Interviewer: So what is it about Southampton in particular that has attracted so many of these sightings do you think? When I was preparing for this interview I was reading that the city has one of the highest amounts of reported sightings in the country, is that correct?

Carl Soter: Absolutely it is. We still struggle to find the exact reason why, but Southampton really seems to attract these things. The city has always had ties with paranormal phenomena as you'll know, but it is incredibly bizarre the amount of UFO reports the Hampshire police receive each year.

Interviewer: Are you often in contact with these people who

[Interrupting]

Carl Soter: Oh yes, I have been working with MUFON (the Mutual Unidentified Flying Object Network) and investigating these cases for years now. I think it's important to take all of these cases seriously. For some people these things can be more than just a sighting you know? It's no surprise also that Southampton has a wonderful local organisation that looks into these reports too. A man named Steve Gerrard runs it and also puts together a monthly newsletter too.

Interviewer: What do these people have to say when they contact you?

Carl Soter: Typically they'll have filled in a form reporting the case and I'll contact them off the back of that.

Interviewer: Are they scared a lot of the time when you're reaching out?

Carl Soter: Sometimes! I mean a lot of the time they're just excited to talk about it. It makes people feel very special when they see something unusual. I always hold off explaining how common they are in this city.

[Laughing]
[AUDIO ENDS]

TRANSCRIPT

The man behind Strange Southampton. Promised anonymity so spoke via phone. I think he used a voice transformer can't be sure. Only knows interested in this as looking into friend's disappeance.

LB: Where did Strange Southampton come from?
SS: I run it so people don't forget about the history of the city. No one else will tell these stories. Everyone else has gone under, demoted to the archives of the internet. They don't want people to know.

LB: Who?
SS: They don't. The authorities. The Government. It goes all the way up.

LB: So what don't they want you to know?
SS: There's paranormal happenings going on - different worlds, different realms. You've read the site right? It's all true. Dark beings, UFOs, disappearances, ageless people - they reach a certain point in their life and that's them, forever. There's a turning point. Then they taunt you - they're just there. On the streets. A reminder that there's more out there than our poxy minds can handle and no one believes you. It's outrageous. What are they here for? Why do they exist? What are they going to do to us? Someone needs to be asking these questions. They do these stupid tours and make our history quirky - our history walks the streets and has done for centuries.

LB: What do you think is happening?
SS: That's what I'm trying to work out. Hundreds of years these legends keep appearing and people say it's all in our heads? No. It's all there. We just need to piece it together. Take the Fair all those years ago. Wrapped in secrecy - 'disrupted' they say. But how? They're hiding something - someone needs to tell the people what they're dealing with.

LB: So why be anonymous if you want people to know?
SS: Don't you wonder why it's just me left? We had hundreds back in the day, all investigating and telling the world what the authorities were too scared to have them know, or would rather keep them in the dark. SUFOG, the others - do you ever wonder what happened to them? They just lose interest? They stop, move away? No. They were threatened, scared, gotten rid of. I won't go the same way. I won't be silenced.

LB: Got rid of?
SS: Are you a sceptic? I'm not here to waste my time with-

LB: No, I'm not... I'm not, just... Someone I know went missing, and you referred to him on the site. James Scythe. He was looking into the same things you were - I want to understand what he saw, what you see.
SS: That investigator guy? I heard he was in town but never managed to find him myself. He went missing? Aren't you listening to me? They did it. The government.

LB: Come on, you seriously-
SS: I'm not here to waste my time with sceptics. Be another sheep. I have work to get on with.

TRANSCRIPT ENDS

Been unable to identify the founder of Strange Southampton. All data encrypted. No further contact – number and email appear to be blocked, no replies since we spoke.

G DURING THE STRANGER WALK

JS: James Scythe
TG: Tour Guide
??: Unidentified walk participants

begins]

JS: I'm heading into the city centre for the Stranger Walk. It's a little after10pm, November 5th 2014. The firework displays are over and the city is clearing out but it's busier than usual. I'm not sure how well audio will be picked up but I'll try to record as much as possible.

[Audio break]

[Muffled speech, assuming from tour guide]

JS: It's quite tourist focused. That's what I'd heard on websites. The Titanic Memorial was moving, The Wool House from the 14th century interesting. I was too far back to completely hear what the guide was saying. It used to house prisoners in the Napoleonic wars according to the plaque. Touristy ghost walk, residential areas and most notably Southampton Docks.

TG: The Bargate was built circa 1180 and was the gateway to the medieval city of Southampton. You can't imagine the people who walked these streets in its almost 1000 years of history. It is said The Stranger used to linger in its shadows, the ghosts and grief surrounding their loss drawing people to him.

Peter: *[Quiet]* Ooh, the Stranger's lurking in the shadows!

??: Shut up, Peter. I swear if you're going to jump at me on every stop I'm le

TG: *[Speakering over participants]* Arundel Tower, one of the highest points i past. Glance up there and sometimes you can see The Stranger, his shadow city before him-

Peter: *[Interrupting]* How do you know The Stranger is a woman?

TG: Well, historically reports have said-

JS: *[Over TG to self]* There are a couple of people holding up the tour. At leas to look around these areas. I've managed to take photos – will have to see if up.

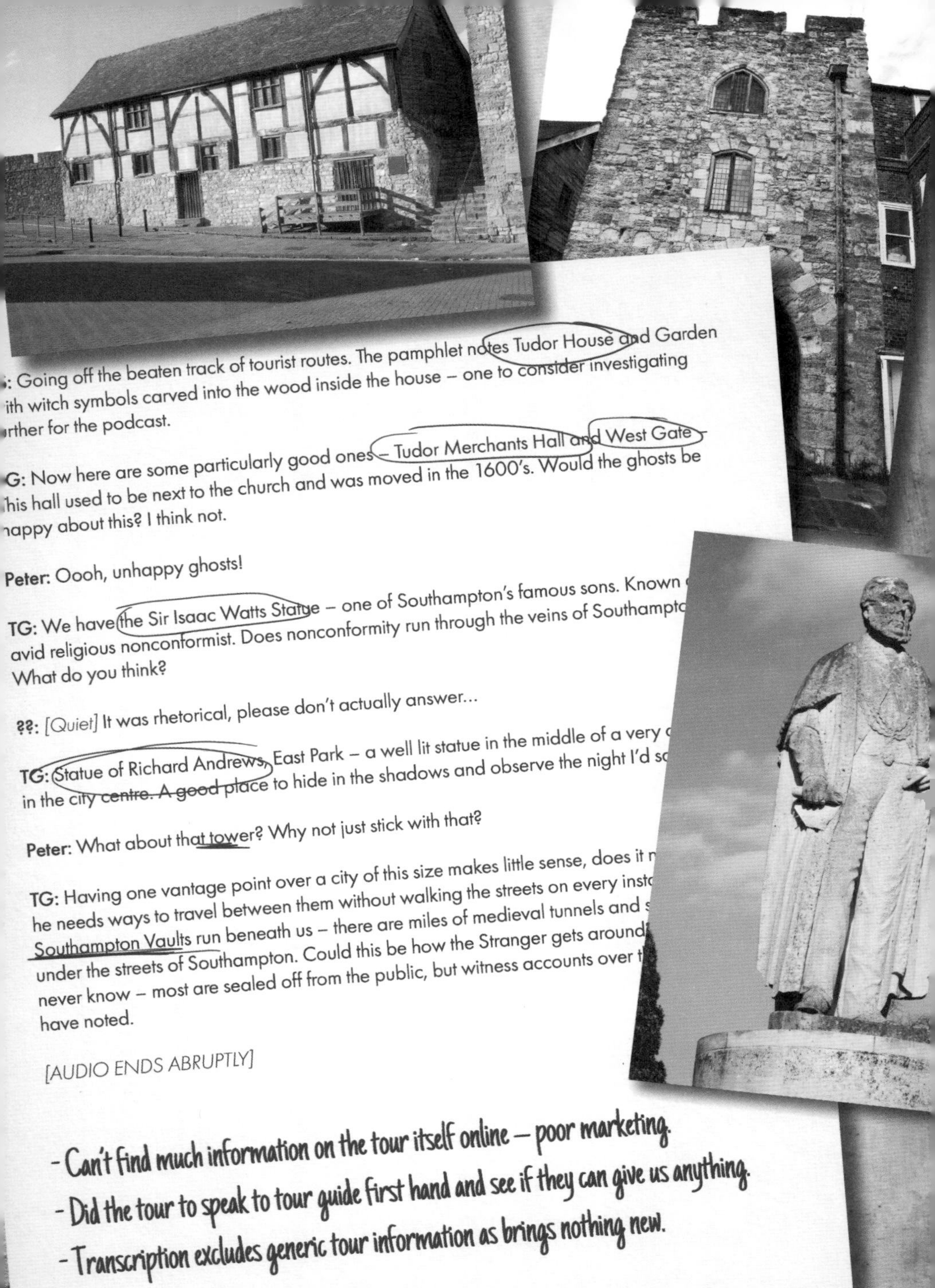

…: Going off the beaten track of tourist routes. The pamphlet notes Tudor House and Garden
…ith witch symbols carved into the wood inside the house – one to consider investigating
…urther for the podcast.
…G: Now here are some particularly good ones – Tudor Merchants Hall and West Gate –
…his hall used to be next to the church and was moved in the 1600's. Would the ghosts be
…happy about this? I think not.
Peter: Oooh, unhappy ghosts!
TG: We have the Sir Isaac Watts Statue – one of Southampton's famous sons. Known …
avid religious nonconformist. Does nonconformity run through the veins of Southampto…
What do you think?
??: [Quiet] It was rhetorical, please don't actually answer...
TG: Statue of Richard Andrews, East Park – a well lit statue in the middle of a very …
in the city ~~centre. A good~~ place to hide in the shadows and observe the night I'd s…
Peter: What about that tower? Why not just stick with that?
TG: Having one vantage point over a city of this size makes little sense, does it …
he needs ways to travel between them without walking the streets on every inst…
Southampton Vaults run beneath us – there are miles of medieval tunnels and …
under the streets of Southampton. Could this be how the Stranger gets around…
never know – most are sealed off from the public, but witness accounts over t…
have noted.
[AUDIO ENDS ABRUPTLY]
- Can't find much information on the tour itself online – poor marketing.
- Did the tour to speak to tour guide first hand and see if they can give us anything.
- Transcription excludes generic tour information as brings nothing new.

TRANSCRIPT: TOUR GUIDE - THEA BLAKE

I managed to join one of the Stranger Walks, though they are less frequent now. I arrived early to be able to ask the tour guide, Thea Blake, some brief questions before we started under the guise of being recommended by James.

LB: Do you mind telling me how you get into this?
TB: I've always been fascinated in the history of the city. I love being able to introduce new people to the happenings of Southampton. There are few jobs where you get to roam streets and tell stories that many would have tried to silence over centuries. We keep them alive. I grew up with these tours and asked to join the moment I could.

LB: Okay, right. A former colleague of mine did this tour a few years back and I wanted to try it out on his recommendation. Do you know who would be working on certain dates? Who might know something about him? James? A slightly common name, I realise.
TB: I couldn't say – we don't really keep records that thorough. Thousands of people do these tours every year, we'll never remember anyone in particular, unless it's a celebrity. We had a few cool authors do the tour a while back, one of them was writing a book on Norse mythology rather than here, so I guess he just liked the culture.

LB: And you really believe in all this?
TB: It's fine if you don't believe, but I do. I believe in history. Do the tour, and you'll see. I'll go see if anyone else is waiting and bring them over.

[footsteps]

Mia: I don't really believe in this either, if it helps. I remember when I was little I heard this interview on Late Night with Lewis that referred to the spooky, UFO shtick in Southampton. So funny. I swore if I ever had the chance I'd do the tours. People seem obsessed, I'd love to see what true believers are like in real life but I'll settle for the spooky spin they put on everything.

LB: An ex-colleague of mine was really into this sort of thing and I'm trying to understand why.
Mia: I guess it's an escapist thing. Nice to imagine there's a potential to live forever, right? Or to escape to another world? I'd kill for a UFO to come fly me away half the time.

LB: That's true. If you could live forever would you really stay here though? *[laughs]*
Mia: I'd go for somewhere warmer I think. Maybe Florida. Would Disneyworld be around forever?

TG: *[Quiet, distant]* Hello ladies and gentlemen and welcome to the Stranger Walk. I warn you now-

LB: I'm Lilly, by the way. I realise I never introduced myself.
Mia: Mia – nice to meet you. Hold on to your socks.

The docks - key part of the tour...

What did James think?

I managed to access the full recording of the "Late Night with Lewis" show Thea was talking about thanks to an unhappy ~~employee~~ at the radio studio who had no qualms with sharing archived recordings. Thank god for disgruntled interns...

TRANSCRIPT OF INTERVIEW WITH JOHN GEORGE, GREW UP WITH 'BELIEVERS' AS PARENTS. FOR LATE NIGHT LOCAL RADIO TALK SHOW 'LATE NIGHTS WITH LEWIS'.

Audio starts at [0:13:09]

Assistant: check, check, one, two. Can you hear me ok there John?

John George: Hi there, yes I can hear you ok

Assistant: Great so I don't know how much they've told you but the plan is for this to go out live on Wednesdays show. The theme this week is "Crazy Childhood", so we've got people telling these stories from their upbringings with extraordinary parents. We've got a girl whose parents were part of a cult, a guy whose Mum dated a ghost and another guy whose parents lived as Klingons, you know like from Star Trek?

John George: Sure

Assistant: So yeah, as you can imagine we're keeping it nice and light. Even though it's going out late, we'd appreciate if you didn't swear on air. But even though it goes out live on Wednesday, it is a pre-record so don't worry too much, we can always get it in the edit.

John George: No problem

Assistant: Ok great, I'm going to connect you with Lewis now and we're just going to go for it if that works with you?

John George: Sure thing

[Long beeping noise]

Lewis (HOST): Hello there John you're live on 'Late Night With Lewis' all across Southampton. How are you this evening?

John George: Hello Lewis, I'm good thank you. How are you?

Lewis (HOST): Not too bad at all. So let's get right down to business, what can you tell us about your Mum and Dad?

John George: Ok so my Mum and Dad were what you'd describe as UFOlogists

Lewis (HOST): That's a term for those people obsessed with 'little green men' right?

TRANSCRIPT OF INTERVIEW WITH JOHN GEORGE, GREW UP WITH

John George: Well it actually is more specifically about unidentified flying objects, but basically yeah you're right.

Lewis (HOST): So tell us John, what was it like growing up with parents like that?

John George: Well it became a bit of a nightmare. When I was a kid it was fine because I didn't know any better you know? But when I started having friends back from school it really weirded them out. My Dad was a part of those silly UFO groups you see around the city all the time. He would talk about it non-stop to anyone who would listen.

Lewis (HOST): These are those nerd groups that meet up and build those tin foil hats right?

[Laughing]

John George: Right. He actually had one of those hats he would wear all the time. They are supposed to stop extra-terrestrials messing with your mind. Imagine bringing back a girlfriend to meet your parents for your first time with him sitting there wearing that.

Lewis (HOST): So hold on, a minute ago you said he was just interested in this 'UFOlogy' topic - which you said was the study of unidentified craft in the sky- and the next you've said he fully believes in extra-terrestrials?

John George: That is exactly what was so messed up about it. Like.. I can understand the interest in a floating light in the sky, but he jumps from that straight to the Aliens thing. It almost felt like he was wants to believe it so bad he puts the pieces of evidence together in a way which he can interpret anyway he likes.

Lewis (HOST): Lets talk about this "evidence" too. What did that consist of?

John George: It was mostly just blurry photos and testimony from crazy ex-military people.

Lewis (HOST): It's funny how photos of these things always seem out of focus

[Laughing]

Lewis (HOST): It's like, c'mon guys. The first thing you should do before you build that silly hat is learn how to take a picture, am I right?

John George: Right!

Lewis (HOST): So what do you make of all of this stuff, John?

John George: Well I it's pretty obvious don't you? I think it's bullshit.

Lewis (HOST): Whoa please watch the language on the air there John. (Speaking to someone off air) We'll have to get that cut out.

John George: I'm sorry Lewis. It's just really strained the relationships with my Mum and my Dad over time. I haven't spoken to them for four years, not even on the phone.

Lewis (HOST): I'm sorry to hear that.

John George: They always talk about how the government is lying to them, that they've seen the truth and how lucky I should feel to have this information. It's crazy man. Like, I'm not a child anymore.

The worst thing is all of it is really just based upon seeing some dumb lights in the sky. Crazy, especially as it's probably all just Chinese lanterns and weather balloons anyway.

Lewis (HOST): Amen to that brother. Well John we're going to let you go but thanks for being on the show tonight.

John George: Thanks for having me Lewis

Lewis (HOST): Not a problem. Thanks also to the George family wherever they are in Southampton. We hope John "phones home" soon.

[AUDIO ENDS]

INTERVIEW WITH SAMANTHA WELSH, UPLOADER OF JAMES SCYTHE'S PODCASTS

[Begins 02m.03s]

LB: Why did you upload the podcasts? And why under his name?
SW: Well he asked someone to keep a copy if they could, so I did. I imagine I'm not the only listener who did that. When he disappeared I didn't know what to do with them but after a while there was a growing interest in what he'd been looking into around Southampton and I thought his podcasts might interest conspirists. Admittedly most of them are messed up now, but still. He was a great researcher, his podcasts were so illuminating. There was a dedicated following to his work, he cut through the nonsense with sense and research. As for his name, why wouldn't I? It's not my work to claim. I hope he'll reappear and take over the account, add to it with more work.

LB: What 'nonesense' was he cutting through?
SW: There's a lot of conspiracy out there, I guess. You feel kind of stupid to talk about a lot of that stuff out loud but I started listening to see what James was doing and found myself really getting hooked.

LB: How did you get hooked?
SW: I knew James from way back, when he'd just met Mary, so, God... Twenty, twenty five years back it must be. We lost touch after they got married. They moved, I moved. I was Googling a few pals from back in the day and discovered he was doing a podcast and thought I'd have a listen.

LB: Oh I knew Mary too, much more recently though. James too, obviously.
SW: Really? She was so nice, wasn't she? Such a shame what happened to her in the end.

LB: Yeah, James wasn't the same after. He sounded very calm in the podcast when I listened, very different to how he'd become at work.
SW: I guess he found his purpose again here – I can only imagine what a loss like that does to you, but believing in something that you know to be true when the world scoffs can make you almost defiant.

LB: Do you know anyone else who follows his podcast? Have you been in touch with anyone since he went missing?
SW: Not really. Most people don't add real names to their accounts, myself included. I feel a bit hypocritical for it but it's easier to keep my name separate. A few people have messaged me asking when the next podcast is going to be uploaded – they generally think I am James, or lose interest when I explain that I'm not, I just wanted to follow his wishes and store the audio files. I'm glad I managed to save the Callous Heart and Stranger files in full, though – I think a few would be quick to jump on his research and claim it as their own, and I suppose that's the other main reason I did it: I want him to get credit where it's due.

LB: So you have no idea what could have happened to James?
SW: My only point of contact was his podcasts, and there's nothing there. I wish I had the answers, but it's almost fitting that he's a mystery in his own right now. He could be timeless like the Callous Heart folks he talks about – maybe we'll have podcasts made about him one day. I mean obviously I would rather he's found safe and happy, but his legacy... at least he's his own story rather than a footnote of someone else's.

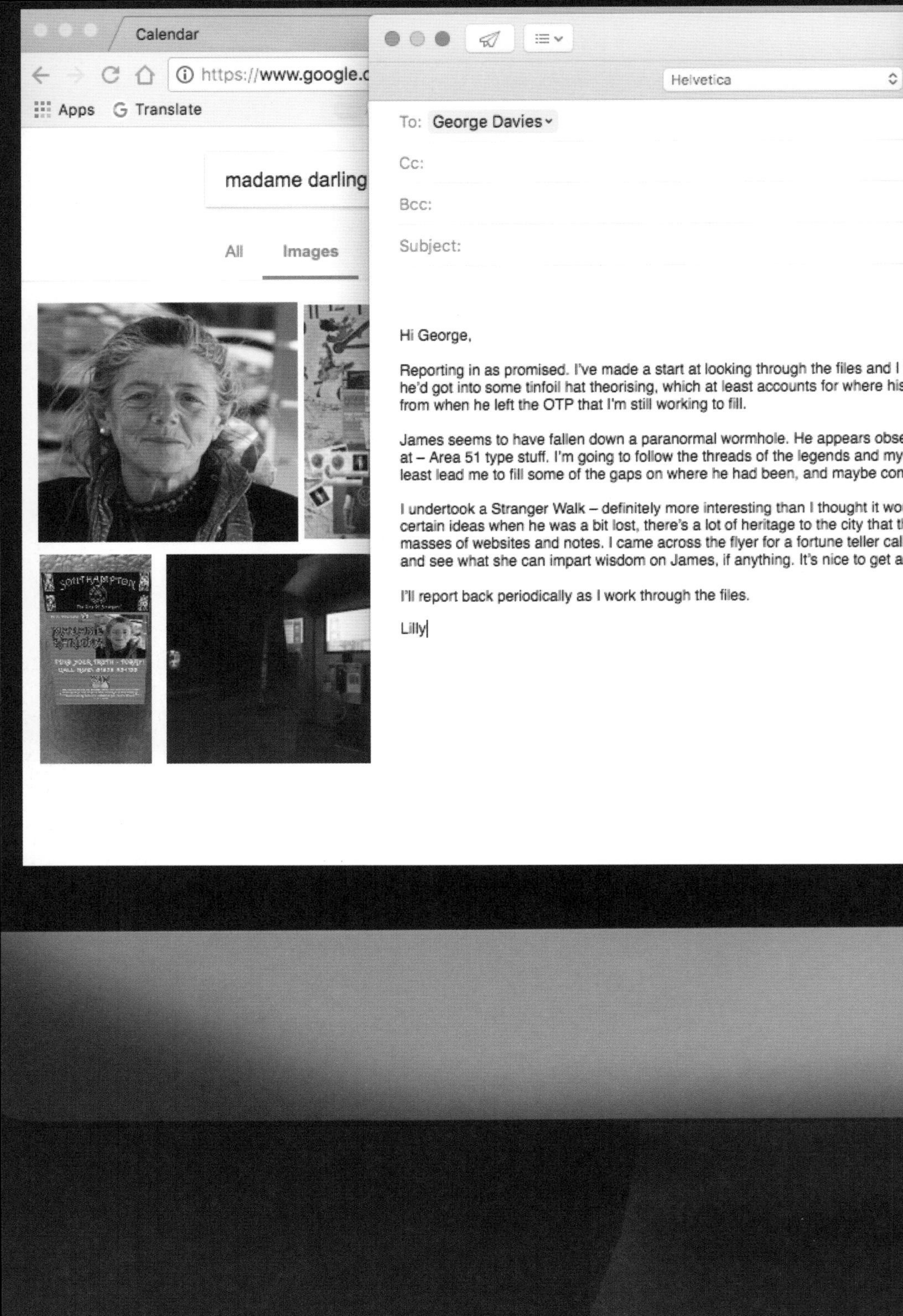
Calendar
https://www.google.c
Apps
Translate
madame darling
All
Images
SOUTHAMPTON
Helvetica
To: George Davies
Cc:
Bcc:
Subject:
Hi George,
Reporting in as promised. I've made a start at looking through the files and I
he'd got into some tinfoil hat theorising, which at least accounts for where his
from when he left the OTP that I'm still working to fill.
James seems to have fallen down a paranormal wormhole. He appears obse
at – Area 51 type stuff. I'm going to follow the threads of the legends and my
least lead me to fill some of the gaps on where he had been, and maybe con
I undertook a Stranger Walk – definitely more interesting than I thought it wo
certain ideas when he was a bit lost, there's a lot of heritage to the city that t
masses of websites and notes. I came across the flyer for a fortune teller cal
and see what she can impart wisdom on James, if anything. It's nice to get a
I'll report back periodically as I work through the files.
Lilly

mes had spiralled far worse than we could have imagined. I'm sorry to say it seems
vas but not what happened to him. There are a lot of unaccounted gaps in his timeline

not sure how much you dove into the files, but his podcast shows where his mind was
most heavily into; he dedicated a lot of time to researching them, so I think this will at
ome others who can shed light on James in his darker years.

of the higher end spook tours I've seen. It was easy to see why he got swept along in
aged to twist to fit their legends, but admittedly it was also a bit of a reprieve in the
e Darling, who James seemed to have visited at some point. I'm going to get a reading
e desk and get some fresh air, clears the head a bit so I can think.

SOUTHAMPTON
PSYCHIC READER
"The City Of Strangers"
#8 in Attractions
MADAME DARLING
FIND YOUR TRUTH - TODAY!
CALL NOW: 01628 904133

"I was lost before visiting Madame Darling: her
helped me get a clear picture ofwhat my long term
Because of her honesty my heart was open and I met
Madame Darling has such a tremendous gift - this is
- J.D. London

12:30AM

I have just returned from the medium I was told about, perhaps the first genuinely solid lead I've had so far. 'Madame Darling' as she went by, was quite difficult to track down and I never did get a real name for her.
I won't reveal her address as I promised not to but I will try to describe it.

I entered through a dimly lit porch and under a low hanging drape into what I can only assume was once a living room. I had the feeling she moved around a lot as bar the drapes over the door, the room was bare.
A single light bulb hung without a shade in the centre of the room above a table.
The place smelt a weird mixture of damp and incense, kind of the way you'd imagine a palm readers bow top wagon might, appropriate.

Madame Darling sat across the table, shuffling a pack of tarot cards as I entered.
She shuffled them over and over again it was almost hypnotic.
I found myself wondering how long she'd been sat there for, hours? Days?
It's hard to describe her appearance as she was covered almost entirely by a purple shawl.

Her mouth and hands were all I could really make out in the light.
Even still, it became frustratingly obvious that the woman pictured on her flyer was not the same woman in front of me. It was a decoy.

The first thing she requested was money, obviously.
"Twenty."
Her voice is hard to describe. It was croaky, accent less, as if she came from nowhere. I'd had experience with these sorts of scams before and knew 'cash up front' was the norm. I slid a £20 note across the table from my purse, which seemed to be some kind of true magic as she finally stopped shuffling for long enough to pick it up.

Another really important thing to mention is that there was no chair for which I could sit on. She sat and I stood for the entire encounter. She went back to shuffling. After an uncomfortable moment's silence she slid the deck across to me and asked me to shuffle. I awkwardly bent down, picked up the purple deck and did as she asked.

All of these theatrics are part of the scam you see. I think she knew exactly what she was doing, trying to put me on edge, to make me jump to conclusions in her reading. I put the deck down and slid it back to her.

She picked three cards from the top of the deck and laid them face down in front of me. Those three cards would be all she would use for the reading, something more in common with a three-card Monte street hustle than a traditional tarot reading. I expect both routines actually have quite a lot in common, each just as exploitative.

Madame Darling first turned over the card on my far right first, revealing 'The Lovers
"You already know what this card means," she said
She was right. I'd read up on tarot prior to my arrival. I knew this card typically
represented the establishment of a personal belief system.
Granted it was strange that she would know this of me, but I put this down to
showmanship.

What was different about this card was the picture of the couple. In traditional tarot
this card typically depicts a non-descript couple holding hands, the couple on Madam
Darlings were wearing jackets similar to what James had been researching.

I will admit I was a little spooked at first, but this is Southampton - home of thes
legends and myths. I decided not to reply.

As she turned over the next card she began speaking before it was even revealed.
"Off we skip like the most heartless things in the world"
he card she turned over was unlike anything I'd seen in my research. It was na
he Stranger' and depicted a hooded demon.
ck-Tock" she whispered
gan to feel uneasy. Not because I was buying in to this routine of hers, but
ng was making any sense.

The Stranger

She sat there staring at this card for a moment in complete silence, not explaining anything. I saw an opportunity in the silence and decided to pounce.

"Mrs Darling, you don't know me but I believe you may know my colleague." There was a pause as her eyes slowly crept up to meet mine and I saw her wrinkled face for the first time. Suddenly I felt terrified. "I need to talk to you about James Scythe" I just about uttered. What happened next I can still not properly explain. "Oh Lilly" she called me by name despite me not giving it to her. "You need to understand something.." Madame Darling picked up the final card and turned it over onto the table. The card was another non-conventional tarot named 'The Inquisitor.' It depicted what looked to be a religious man wearing a plague doctor mask with a hook for a hand. "All of this has happened before, and it will all happen again."

I quickly grabbed all three of the cards and ran. She sat in silence, almost letting me. I ripped open the drapes and dashed out onto the Southampton street and back to my hotel. That is where I write from tonight. I feel kind of silly in hindsight; the cards have a disarming cartoonish vibe to them almost. They don't seem nearly as imposing as they did for that split second.

I think I need to sleep; I need to stop working this case at night.
The thing is it always seems so dark here I have no idea why.
Either way, I suppose today was eventful one.
I will keep you updated.

L

THE CALLOUS HEART

TRACED BACK TO 18TH CENTURY — EYEWITNESS REPORTS AND STORIES PRINTED IN LOCAL NEWSPAPERS — ECHO DAILY. (PROUD OF THE GROUP?) REPORTS: STREET YOUTHS WEARING DEATHS HEAD INSIGNIAS ON CLOTHES FURTHER BACK.

NO CONFIRMED PHOTOS — ONE ACCOUNT 'CAMERA FILM GONE BAD' WHEN SNAPPED.

DESCRIPTIONS OF EMBLEM: DEATHS HEAD REAPER WITH SCYTHE IN HEART. GRAFFITI ON BACK OF SOUTHAMPTON SIGN – 'BEWARE THE CALLOUS HEART' SEEN IN SOME BAND'S VIDEO. ????

EXCLUSIVELY YOUNG — NO SENIOR RANKING OR ADULTS WEARING THIS. NO INFRASTRUCTURE TO MEMBERSHIP — LIKE VICTORIAN CRIME GANGS OR MOTORCYCLE CLUBS 1960S

WHO ARE THEY?? WHAT DO THEY DO??

THE CALLOUS HEART DO NOT AGE. FOREVER YOUNG. CONNECTED TO EXTRA TERRESTRIAL PRESENCE?? SPECULATION

WHO ARE THEY??

UPDATE ON SS - 26 DEC 15

BAND USING EMBLEM. SEEMS UNRELATED 'ART CRUDELY IMITATING LIFE'

'FORMER INVESTIGATOR FROM THE OFFICE OF OTP ("OMBUDSMEN OF THE PRETERNATURAL") ARRIVED IN SOUTHAMPTON AND HAS BEEN ASKING QUESTIONS ABOUT BOTH TCH AND ANOTHER CITY LEGEND THE STRANGER. S GOING TO TRY FIND - JAMES??

UPDATE ON SS - 15 JAN 16

NOT FOUND 'JAMES'. ANOTHER UPDATE RE: TCH BUT IRRELEVANT TO THIS. WHERE DID THEY HEAR ABOUT JAMES BEING IN TOWN? KEEP TRYING TO FIND.

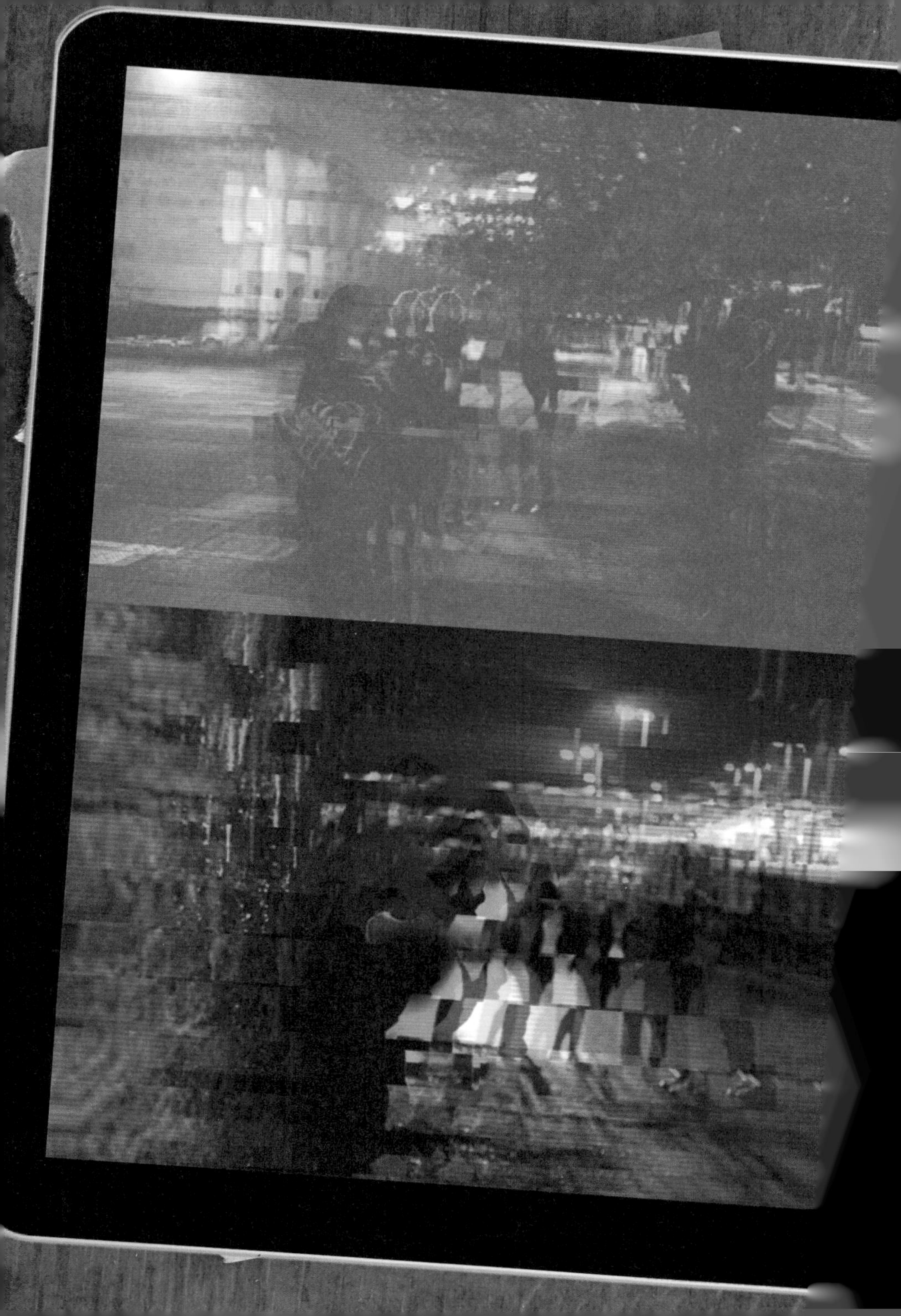

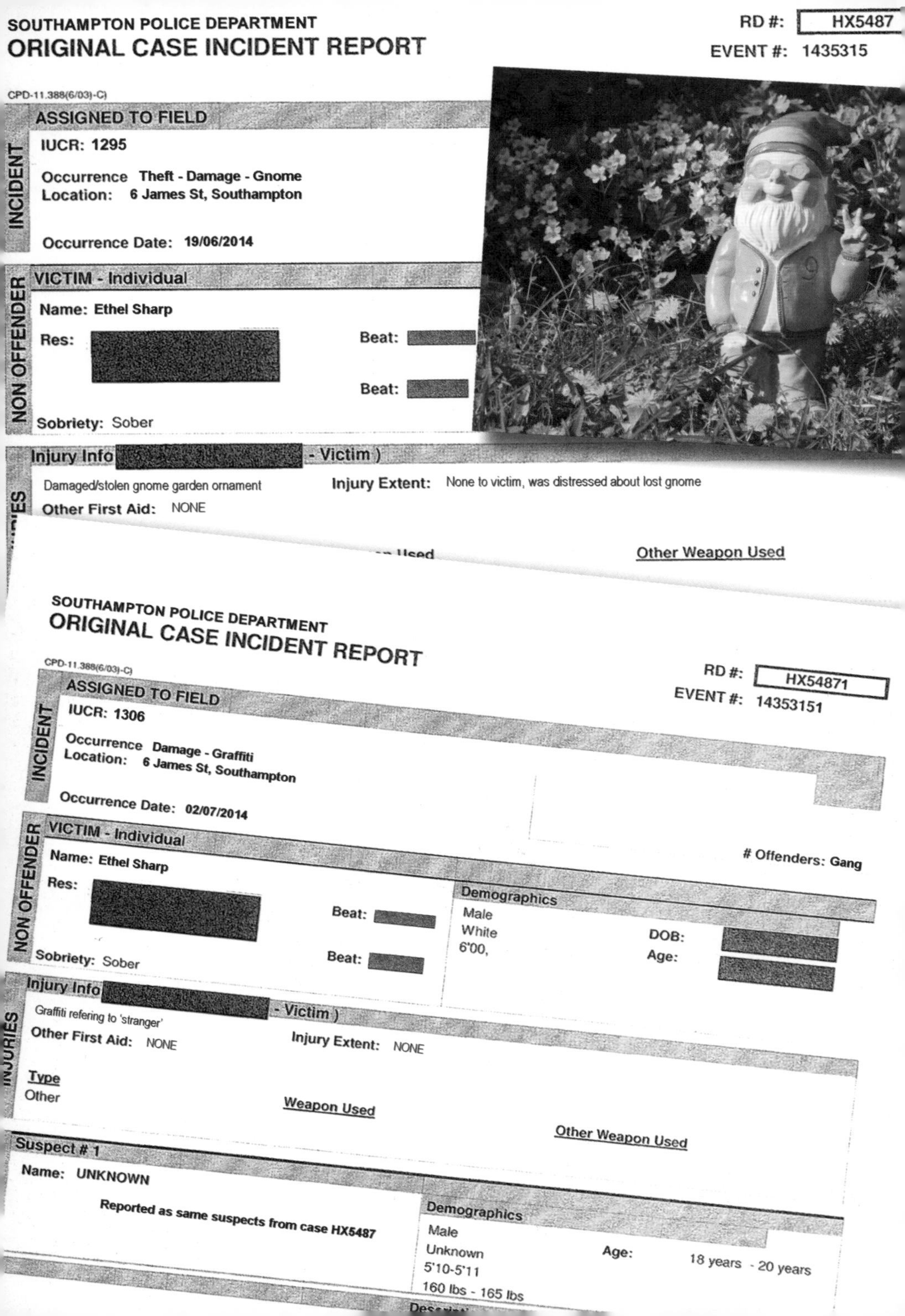

SOUTHAMPTON POLICE DEPARTMENT

ORIGINAL CASE INCIDENT REPORT

RD #: HX5487

EVENT #: 1435315

CPD-11.388(6/03)-C)

INCIDENT

ASSIGNED TO FIELD

IUCR: 1295

Occurrence Theft - Damage - Gnome

Location: 6 James St, Southampton

Occurrence Date: 19/06/2014

NON OFFENDER

VICTIM - Individual

Name: Ethel Sharp

Res: [redacted]

Beat: [redacted]

Beat: [redacted]

Sobriety: Sober

INJURIES

Injury Info [redacted] - Victim)

Damaged/stolen gnome garden ornament

Injury Extent: None to victim, was distressed about lost gnome

Other First Aid: NONE

...n Used

Other Weapon Used

SOUTHAMPTON POLICE DEPARTMENT

ORIGINAL CASE INCIDENT REPORT

CPD-11.388(6/03)-C)

RD #: HX54871

EVENT #: 14353151

INCIDENT

ASSIGNED TO FIELD

IUCR: 1306

Occurrence Damage - Graffiti

Location: 6 James St, Southampton

Occurrence Date: 02/07/2014

NON OFFENDER

VICTIM - Individual

Name: Ethel Sharp

Offenders: Gang

Res: [redacted]

Beat: [redacted]

Beat: [redacted]

Sobriety: Sober

Demographics

Male

White

6'00,

DOB: [redacted]

Age: [redacted]

INJURIES

Injury Info [redacted] - Victim)

Graffiti refering to 'stranger'

Other First Aid: NONE

Injury Extent: NONE

Type

Other

Weapon Used

Other Weapon Used

Suspect # 1

Name: UNKNOWN

Reported as same suspects from case HX5487

Demographics

Male

Unknown

5'10-5'11

160 lbs - 165 lbs

Age: 18 years - 20 years

Community Courier Southampton

A community that cares in the cruise capital of Europe

March, 2014

Inside this issue

LOCAL THEFTS!

THE COMMUNITY IS APPEALING for information about a robbery on Captains Place in Southampton on the evening of March 9th. Bill Green, reported that a number of rare books and old family documents had been stolen. The police are currently pursuing leads as to whether these books are being sold, and have so far found no information as to the perpetrators via CCTV.

Books taken from the home include first editions of: The Time Machine, H.G. Wells; The Women in White, Wilkie Collins; The Strange Case of Dr Jekyll and Mr Hyde, Robert Louis Stevenson, and The Vicar of Nibbleswicke by Roald Dahl.

In order to feel safe in our homes we need to keep our eyes out and remain vigilant to protect not just our own homes, but thos[e] around us. One of our

They're trouble. I report them continuously for loitering and the police do nothing. Who else would it be? You think the Vicar is roaming the streets stealing from his parishioners? This is an upstanding neighbourhood, and interlopers won't be tolerated. If you have any information please do get in touch and make our homes safer."

Please note, this remains speculation at this point, but with weeks of no information, hopefully this can be jump off point of solving this. If you have any information please get in touch with your neighbourhood representative and it will be passed along.

Note: Ethel Sharp is one of numerous funders of The Community Courier, and submitted her own statement for the article.

NOME THEFT

mber of anti-social incidents have been
ted to local police following graffiti on
s St, bins set on fire and, in one in-
e, a garden gnome being stolen. The
n, choosing to remain anonymous, put
ame on a group of youths. "They hang
d looking to cause trouble in their
ing clothing with what looks like
on their jackets. We shou

INTERVIEW WITH CALUM BRODERICK - CALLOUS HEART OBSESSIVE

JS: Thanks for agreeing to talk to me, I shouldn't keep you too long. The Community Courier let slip your name when I was talking to them and wouldn't tell me any more, it was quite hard to track you down. Common name and all that...
CB: It's no problem, I'm just walking home just now to got a few minutes to kill - as far as I know I'm the only one who responded to their stupid article. I wanted to set the record straight so I'm glad I get to in some way.

JS: Set it straight? What did they get wrong? What information did you give them?
CB: That it wasn't The Callous Heart. They have a grudge against them. It creeps up a lot from that Ethel woman but blaming them for a crime, I couldn't sit by. For one, that Green fella notoriously brags about all the cool stuff he owns. There's a list as long as one of those books of people who could steal that - but Ethel running her propaganda rag again-

JS: Propaganda rag is a bit strong for a neighbourhood watch...
CB: Yeah, yeah, sure. Come in with your big city sensibilities and laugh - the Courier is a dictatorship, and Ethel just goes on and on, saying what she wants, pointing fingers for every happening in the neighbourhood. We all see her do it, and everyone keeps their mouth shut. I can't do that when it comes to The Callous Heart being blamed again.

JS: Okay, sorry. So how do you know it wasn't The Callous Heart? If he brags a lot, it could be anyone.
CB: Because I was with them. I am one of them. I followed them for a while, but recently we've grown apart.

JS: How old are you?
CB: 21. Just turned.

JS: They're a bit younger than you, no? What can you tell me about The Callous Heart?
CB: No, we're all different ages. And what do you want to know? We're just friends who hang out, wander around the streets. Is that a crime?

JS: They've got quite a reputation as more than just a group of friends, though.

CB: That's true, we do have quite a reputation. I don't know, we just hang out. Some come, some go. It's been going for decades. You get introduced via a secret code, I obviously can't tell you that, and once you're in, you're until it's your time to let the new ones in. We wander the streets, chat, nothing fancy. No grand adventures or crime sprees.

JS: But the rumours say that they're the same people, and not just a rotating club across the decades.

REALLY??

CB: I'm evidence that that's not true!

DONT THINK SO

JS: How did you first discover The Callous Heart?

CB: Just always been aware of them - they've always been around, cult like following. When I was younger I used to dream of being part of them, wished I was that cool [illegible] anything to- Uh, then getting to be involved was amazing. Guess they must seek out the true believers and lucky me, I'm [illegible]

SEEMS TO BE DEFLECTING

DONT THINK HE KNOWS WHAT HE IS TALKING ABOUT?

JS: Believers in what?

CB: I'm losing track of what we're talking about to be honest.

JS: Right... So who else is in The Callous Heart? With you?

CB: I can't tell you that. All secret, ain't it. You can tell us by the jackets we wear. I still wear mine, not quite ready to let it go yet. Greatest years of my life.

JS: The logo does look slightly different to the descriptions...

CB: Look dude, you wanted to talk to me about the rag and we're getting off topic. The Callous Heart are innocent, and unless you become one of us, you'll never get the secrets of us. Comes with the territory. I'm nearly home so keep it on topic or I'm out.

JS: Okay, then - what else have they been blamed for in the Courier?

CB: Graffiti, arsons, noise, pretty much anything that happens. Ethel's out there pointing the finger at them. Swear she has posters of them up in her house that she throws darts at. They post wanted drawings of them all the time in the rag. It's a vendetta. She doesn't care for the neighbourhood, or facts.

JS: Okay, thanks for that.

CB: Do you believe that they did that stupid robbery?

JS: Not really, no, from everything I've heard about them-

CB: Good, then my job here is done. I gotta go.

CALL ENDS

locate?

1/4/15

SPOKE TO CALUM BRODERICK, CALLOUS HEART
MEMBER, CRITIC OF THE COMMUNITY COURIER
IRRITABLE WHEN QUESTIONED TO BACK ANYTHING HE
CLAMED UP UP. IRONICALLY MYSELF BELIEVING PA
OF WHAT HE SAID, BUT SEEMED TO DRILL HARD THAT
WAS A MEMBER ABOVE ALL ELSE UNUSUAL, OF
TCH MEMBERS ARE VIRTUALLY IMPOSSIBLE TO TRAC
RUMOURED PEOPLE INVOLVED COMPLETELY SHUT O
EXTERNAL CONTACT. JILTED TCH MEMBER? FAN??

Did he actually find any?

CAN'T SEE TCH BEING INTERESTED IN VINTAGE BOOKS
DOESN'T FIT THE MOULD OF ANYTHING READ SO FAR

TRIED TO REACH OUT TO MR BILL GREEN: ASKED IF
HAD MADE ANY HEADWAY WITH THE CASE, OR IF HE HA
SEEN THE ARTICLE IN THE COMMUNITY COURIER AND
THOUGHTS ON IT. TOLD TO GET LOST (IN A FAR LESS
PLEASANT WAY).

TRIED TO REACH OUT TO POLICE: STANDARD RESPON
INVESTIGATION ONGOING. ANY INFORMATION THAT CAN
PUBLIC IS, NO KEY SUSPECTS, AS STATED ELSEWHE
PROBED ABOUT TCH, PERSON ON PHONE LAUGHED A
REPEATED PREVIOUS LINES.

NEXT GOAL: TRY TO REACH ETHEL SHARP. (~~QUEEN OF~~
~~LOCAL PROPAGANDA RAG!!!~~) (NEIGHBOURHOOD WAT
COMMUNITY COURIER)

Followed up: Books never found, insurance paid out. No comment from Green.

Case closed, had no comment

PROPERTY
OF OTP

8/4/15

TODAY WAS UNEVENTFUL. I CURLED UP WITH A GOOD BOOK (THE HITCHHIKER'S GUIDE) AND DISTRACTED MYSELF FROM THE MOUNTAIN OF WORK I KNOW I NEED TO DO. THAT'S THE PROBLEM WITH BEING YOUR OWN BOSS, NO ONE TO KICK ME INTO LINE WHEN DISTRACTIONS ARISE. MARY ALWAYS GABBED ON ABOUT THIS BOOK, I NEVER GOT HER "THANKS FOR ALL THE FISH" REFERENCES WHEN PEOPLE WOULD SAY GOODBYE. IT SEEMS I OWE IT TO HER TO FINALLY GET AROUND TO IT. SO FAR SO GOOD. SHE ALWAYS KNEW BEST.

11/4/15

I SAW HER? I'VE BEEN DIGGING AROUND INTO SOUTHAMPTON'S MYTHS AND LEGENDS, I'D READ THE RUMOURS OF THE CALLOUS HEART THROUGH MY RESEARCH BUT... THIS MAKES NO SENSE. I DON'T KNOW HOW TO SAY IT, EVEN ON PAPER, EVEN JUST FOR MYSELF. I'VE BEEN TRYING TO CATCH SIGHTS OF THE GROUP AROUND THE CITY AND SHE WAS... THERE. HER HAIR WAS DIFFERENT BUT HER FACE, THAT SMILE. HOW IS THAT POSSIBLE? MARY? IT'S BEEN YEARS.
I WATCHED YOU DIE.
I AM TERRIFIED, BUT FULL OF WONDER

INTERVIEW WITH ETHEL SHARP - TRANSCRIPT

[GREETINGS OMITTED]

ES: Yes, that all sounds good, I have plenty to say.

JS: Great, thank you. So as I explained I wanted to talk to you about the article in The Community Courier regarding Mr Green's robbery and some accusations you made in it. Could you start with the night of the robbery?
ES: I was watching reruns of Murder, She Wrote. Or it might have been my own taping. Either way I was watching Murder, She Wrote as usual. I heard noise outside, couldn't tell you the time, and it was that group laughing and cackling away as they always do. So much noise. It's as if they want us to catch them.

JS: The Callous Heart?
ES: If that's what they call themselves, but they're no better than a gang. It's the same group that have been bothering us for years. They cause trouble endlessly and somehow they get away with it. So dark and shadowy, would it kill them to wear some colour and go get a hobby? I've been retired for several years but my cause now is to keep this neighbourhood safe. We just want peace and quiet. We work hard to have a nice and friendly neighbourhood, and they wreck it. At first we thought they'd grow up and leave us alone, but it seems like that's not the case.

JS: What have they done to you?
ES: What haven't they? They stole Mr Green's books, probably to sell on these shady underground markets for who knows what. I've lived here decades and we never had any trouble, then a few years ago around the first time I saw them in the Captain's area, we had graffiti. Graffiti! Some young team nonsense. There's been bins set on fire, petty thefts from gardens. Did you know Gloria lost her prize gnome the other year?

JS: No I didn't. That's a shame for Gloria... How often does something occur in the neighbourhood?
ES: I'd say at least a dozen incidents in the last few years. But one is too many.

JS: Okay. I've been unable to find previous issues of the paper but I wondered how much this group featured in it?
ES: Not as often as I'd like - a few times over the years. We always presented the incidents in full detail and reported our suspicions to the police to no avail, then we started to take it into our own hands when we felt it appropriate. The bin on fire for example was horrifying - scared a few of our neighbours in

in particular – but it didn't directly hit them. When Mr Broad at number 17 had his car scratched, that's when we first got the call out for the gang and sourced our own posters as the police were next to useless. All this CCTV and they say "because no one saw them there, we can't do anything". I ask again, who else?

JS: Do you have a copy of those posters I could see at all?
ES: Of course. I don't know if I have the actual poster but I still have the sketches put together if you'd like to see them? You'll have to get copies organised yourself. No idea where to start with there.

JS: That would be great, thank you. So back to the night of the robbery in particular – if you don't know the exact time you heard them, how can you be sure it was them? They could have just been passing by.
ES: I know my neighbourhood, Mr Scythe. I know who doesn't belong here, I know who's up to no good. They were up to no good.

JS: But if you didn't see them–
ES: Mr Scythe, I understand you need to ask your questions, but I know who belongs in this neighbourhood, and who does not.

JS: Okay, understood. I apologise. Have you seen them around since?
ES: Just as frequently as usual! So brazen. They don't care that they've been shamed in our paper, they still galivant around, joking and laughing at us.

JS: Have you ever spoken to any of them?
ES: I've spoken at them – yelled at them to get away from here and find somewhere else to go. I don't know anyone who's actually spoken to them – they just kind of smile and wander off. One waved at me once when I shouted from the window – so rude.

JS: Do you have any leads on their identities then, if you've not spoken to them?
ES: No, other than our posters. No one ever gets in touch except for that one idiot who defends them mercilessly. You don't know them, they wouldn't do that. Ever since that article that's all we hear. Never see him around with them, so no idea why he's so keen to defend them. Sure they'd let him take the fall if he dared show face. They don't seem like honest people. Have you ever spoken to them?

JS: Um, no – I've tried to catch som
only seen them wandering th
them, I don't know
face to fa

ES: If you don't mind me asking, why are you so interested in them if they've not wronged your neighbourhood?

JS: That's a long story [laughs]. Probably best to end things there, we can save that one for another time maybe.

ES: If you do have cause to talk to them, please do let them kn
that I will find them and stop them.

James managed to secure copies of sketches
of TCH following his meeting with Ethel,
and one of them is undeniably Mary.
I don't know how that is possible.

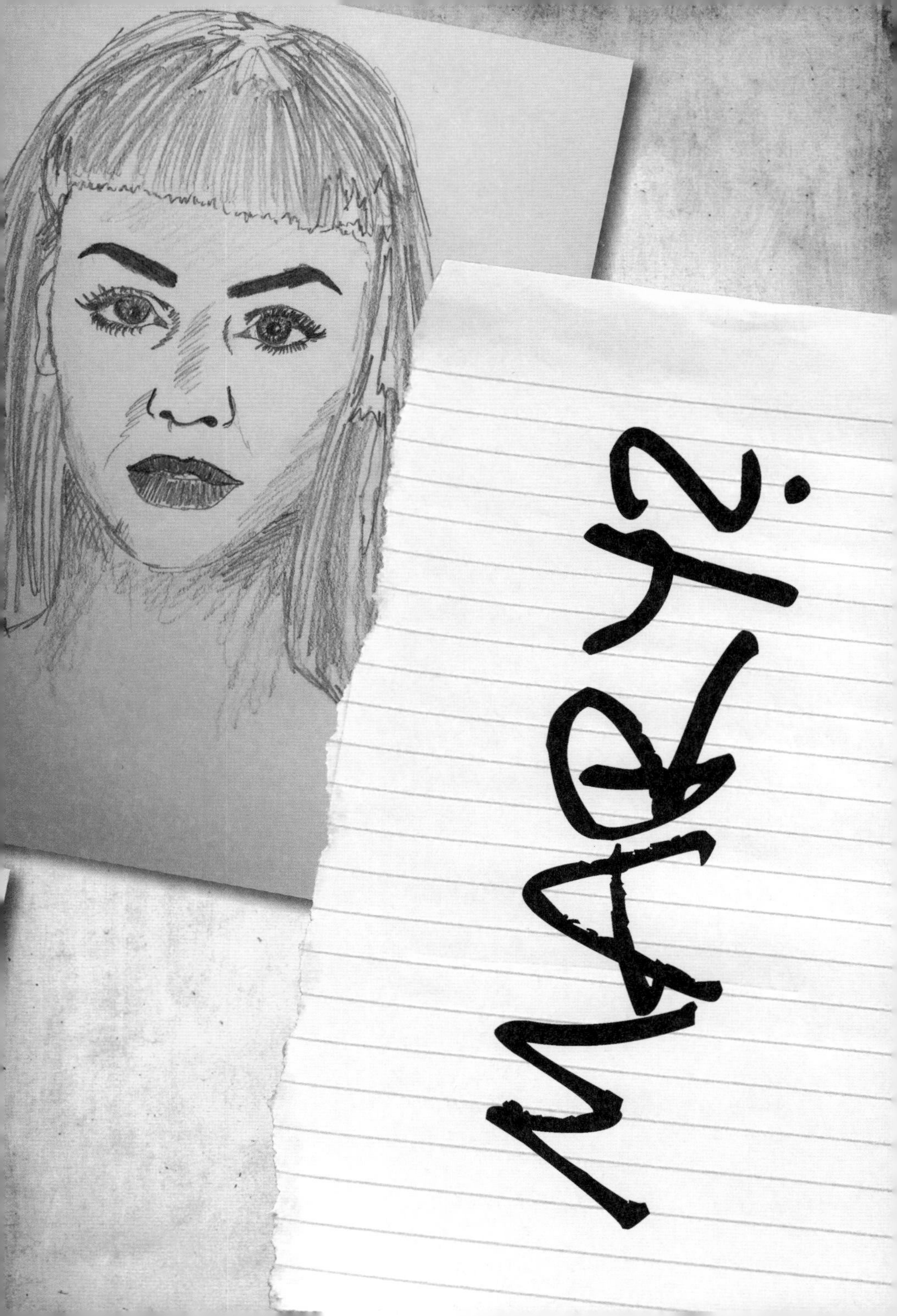
MARY?

November 16 1979

Today I awoke to the sound of the bells of St Michael's Church. We'd slept all day by the old Tudor House. It gets dark early now, the perfect time of year for us. Southampton is so beautiful in the dark.

Lately it feels like we're becoming less and less attatched to the real world. We spent last night atop a roof looking down at the drunks and thugs as they sauntered through the high street. I think the leader is looking for fresh meat, new members to join the cause.

It got me thinking about the lives those people lead. Normal lives, normal jobs, normal houses and normal families. Looking down on the street I could almost remember what it was like to have my own. But this is my family now.

Later a fight broke out between two drunks. A couple of us wanted to get involved but as always it's a democracy and we opted to stay hidden. It's that sort of impending danger and recklessness that surrounds the group all the time, only there's no consequence. We always win.

fter some time we walked down the dock and along
small pier. We stole some cigarettes from a local shop
d sat chaining them on a bench. The leader
oke about the college that was being built. He thinks
at it will attract a number of young people who
ld be beneficial to us.

Suddenly a flash of light went off behind us.
terrified older man with a Kodak trembled. He
pologized. The leader glared and smiled. The man
d a young girl with him and pulled her away
t the girl was looking right at me. Staring
ght into my eyes. So beautiful with long black
air and porcelain skin. She was totally unafraid.
he old man pulled her away and moved
ervously into the distance. I was stunned.
or a moment I almost felt human. At least
he has the photo her Dad randomly took.

Besides, as the leader reminded us, that
hoto will definitely not develop.

Who would have thought that living forever
ould have you feeling so truly dead inside?

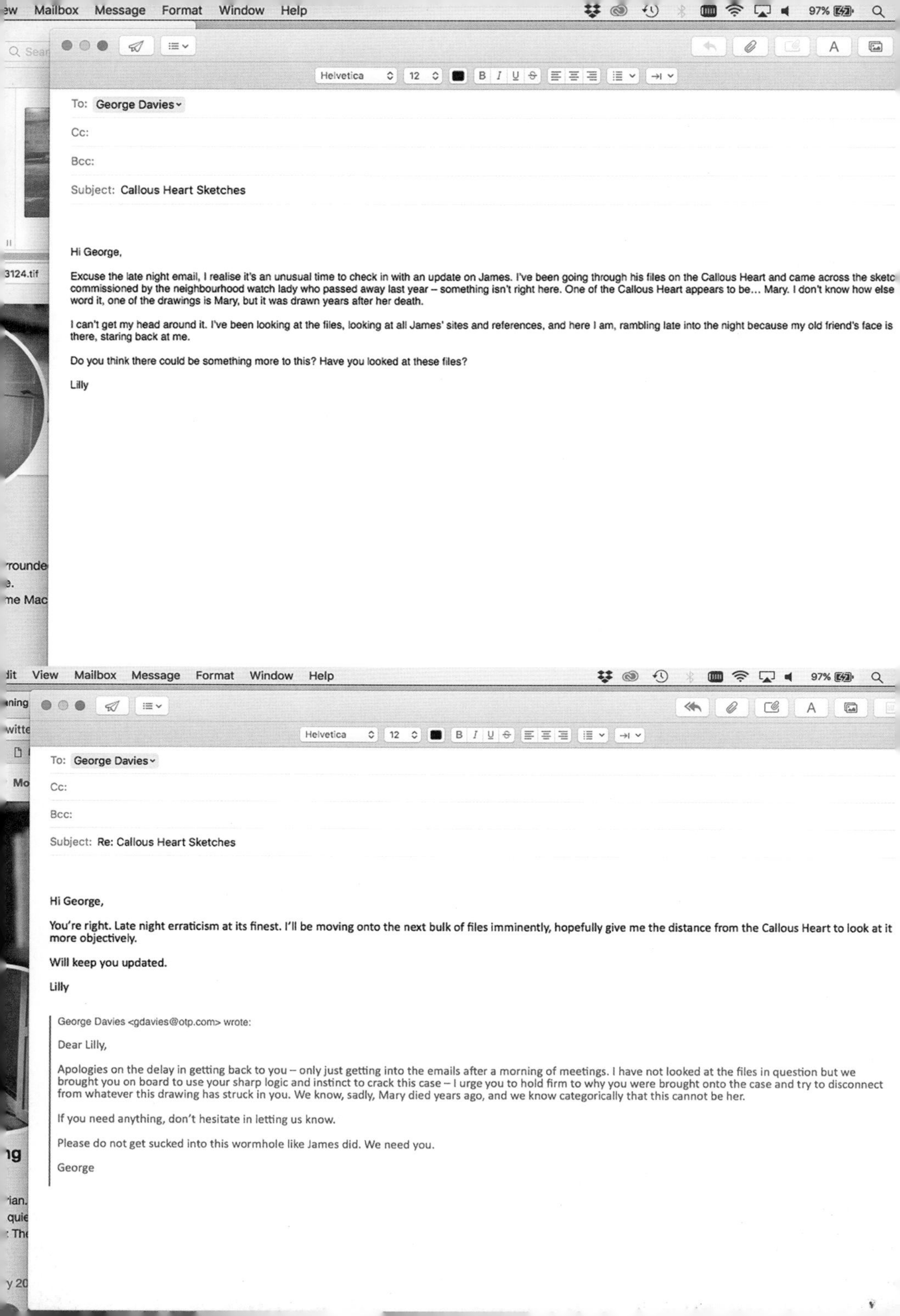

To: George Davies

Cc:

Bcc:

Subject: Callous Heart Sketches

Hi George,

Excuse the late night email, I realise it's an unusual time to check in with an update on James. I've been going through his files on the Callous Heart and came across the sketc commissioned by the neighbourhood watch lady who passed away last year – something isn't right here. One of the Callous Heart appears to be… Mary. I don't know how else word it, one of the drawings is Mary, but it was drawn years after her death.

I can't get my head around it. I've been looking at the files, looking at all James' sites and references, and here I am, rambling late into the night because my old friend's face is there, staring back at me.

Do you think there could be something more to this? Have you looked at these files?

Lilly

To: George Davies

Cc:

Bcc:

Subject: Re: Callous Heart Sketches

Hi George,

You're right. Late night erraticism at its finest. I'll be moving onto the next bulk of files imminently, hopefully give me the distance from the Callous Heart to look at it more objectively.

Will keep you updated.

Lilly

> George Davies <gdavies@otp.com> wrote:
>
> Dear Lilly,
>
> Apologies on the delay in getting back to you – only just getting into the emails after a morning of meetings. I have not looked at the files in question but we brought you on board to use your sharp logic and instinct to crack this case – I urge you to hold firm to why you were brought onto the case and try to disconnect from whatever this drawing has struck in you. We know, sadly, Mary died years ago, and we know categorically that this cannot be her.
>
> If you need anything, don't hesitate in letting us know.
>
> Please do not get sucked into this wormhole like James did. We need you.
>
> George

MEETING WITH CALUM BRODERICK, THE PAN CAFE, APRIL 2017

CB: I don't know what you want me to tell you. I don't know anything about your friend other than that one time we spoke.

LB: I'm not here to talk to you about James, I wanted to talk to you about The Callous Heart.
CB: I mean, I'm fine to talk about The Callous Heart but you said-

LB: Tell me what you know about these people.
CB: The Callous Heart?

LB: These individual people. Each and every one. I guess they're The Callous Heart, but I need more specifics.
CB: I don't recognise any of them. Well, I recognise one or two but I don't really know them.

LB: Tell me.
CB: I recognise these two, I've seen them around, him with the forehead and this one. The others I don't know.

LB: Who are they? What are their names? Where can I find them?
CB: I don't know. Look, I don't know what you want me to tell you.

LB: You told James you were part of The Callous Heart. You're going to tell me you really don't know them? Who is she?
CB: I have no idea. It's been years...

LB: What was Mary doing with you?
CB: Who is-

LB: Enough. [thud] Why was Mary there? She can't have been...
CB: Look lady, I don't know what you want me to tell you. I don't know who Mary is.

LB: Her.
CB: Tap the drawing all you want, I don't know what you want me to say. I don't know who that is.

LB: She was my friend.
CB: And so was this other dude you lied about needing to talk to me about. Lots of f
to have that I know nothing about. Go find The Callous Heart yourself if
talk to them.

LB: But you know them, you are ...
CB: Yeah, I was, uh, but...

LB: I just need to know what happened to

[Stopped recording here]

I followed Broderick after he stormed out, tried to get a photo of him but he ran, only managed to get a shot of his back

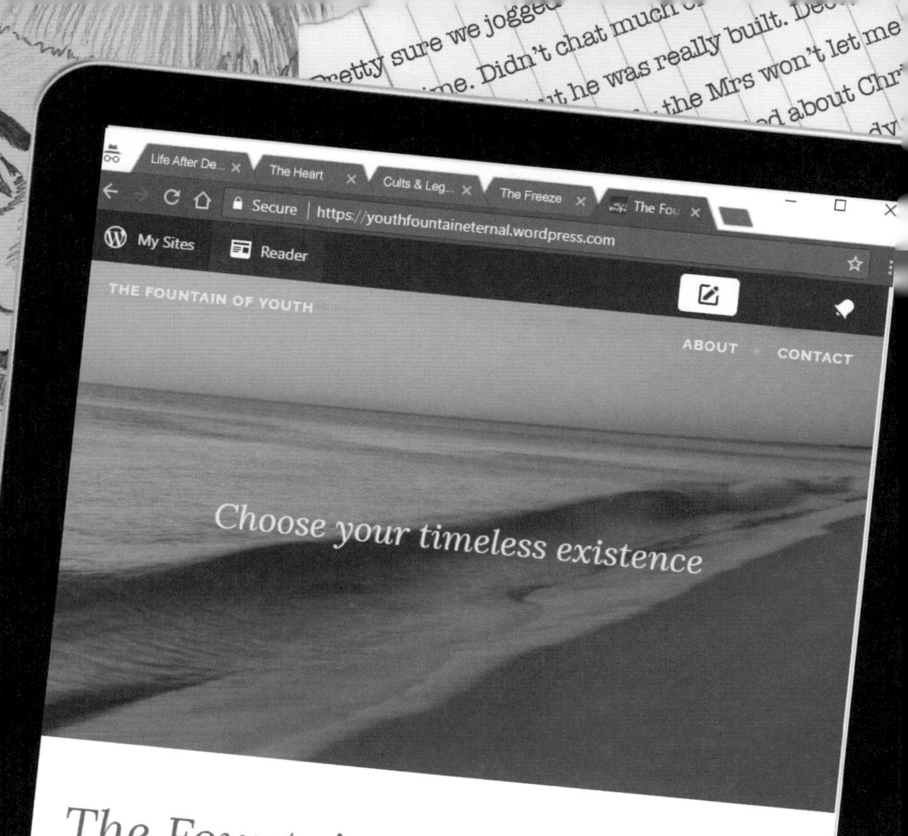

The Fountain of Youth

The Fountain of Youth, or Eternal Life, depending on when you want the freeze to occur. Can you make it happen? Many have tried but few have truly succeeded. Those chosen for a timeless existence rarely speak out about it, which is problematic for developing research, but we persevere in search of a greater truth.

We have compiled as much information and research as possible in these pages on the various stages of Eternal Life. We have broken these into three stages: Youth | Adult | Elder. The lines continually blur, but for organisations this felt the easiest way to divide.

THE YOUTH

One such gang is The Callous Heart, said to be a youthful gang who have roamed the same city streets of Southampton for decades, perhaps centuries depending on where you look. Little information on joining the gang has been discerned though the same descriptions appear to match – they've always had a heart, Reaper, scythe, moon in some form on their attire. Youth seems to be a key characteristic, but new research suggests that adults

Research conducted into eternal life. Mr Granters suggests that proximity to death and grief ties together all examples he has seen.

Elvia, historic case, lost entire family in massacre. Many said she roamed the town as a ghost, but theory that she never died, stayed young innocent self. No body found.

Norman. 1960s. Witnessed incident at local Fair, location unknown. Kept minimal diary, notes for week: 'busy, traumatic, blood' Late 20s at time. Photos over decades, no signs of age.

Callous Heart – no proven members of TCH tracked. Those who claim to be part of it often falter around its eternal legacy. Interviewed decades apart, most clearly age and maintain story that they were involved, or admit made it up. Theory of fake CH for people who wanted to be involved but couldn't get to them.

New research – look into.

Am I still on the right track? I need a fresh angle.

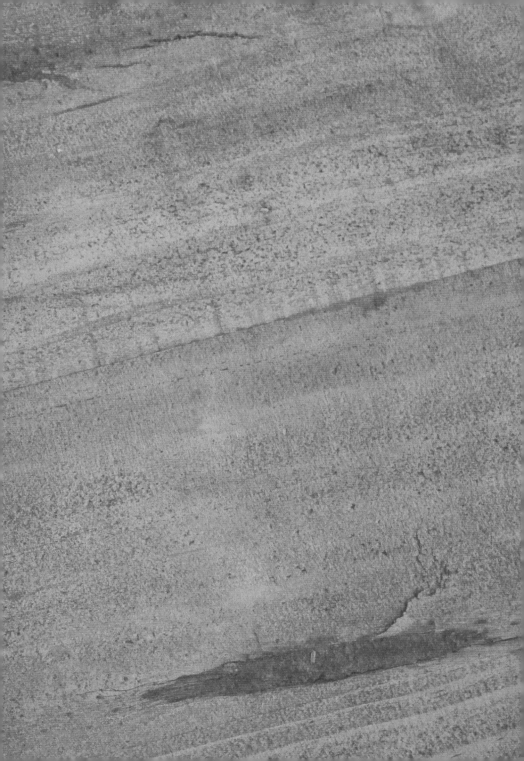

THE STRANGER

SOUTHAMPTON PROUD OF 'MYTH' – HAS STRANGER WALK. STANDARD TOURISTY GHOSTWALK BUT MOSTLY RESIDENTIAL AREAS BOOK TO DO WALK ASAP

STRANGER STORIES: INVOLVE VISITS AT NIGHT FROM ABNORMALLY TALL CLOAKED CHARACTER. PALE SKELETON FACE. KNOWN TO SPEAK IN V LOW TONE, MOUTH DOESN'T MOVE. SIGHTINGS LINKED WITH FEAR AND GRIEF??

1850 – MICHAEL BERNARD (SOTON). 1962: MRS JULIA BENTON (WHEN IN SOUTHAMPTON). BOOK OF DEMONOLOGY – ROBED WATCHER, STRANGE VOYEUR, A BLACK MASS SEEN O'ER HER BED. FIND ARTICLES

ACCOUNTS DATE TO EDWARDIAN PERIOD / TITANIC – DEMONOLOGISTS/SCHOLARS OF DARK FOLKLORE TIE TO SUBSTANTIAL FOG OF GRIEF. SHARED SUFFERING > MASS HALLUCINATIONS?? SIGHTINGS HIGHER AROUND UNDERCROFT VAULT AND TUDOR HOUSE

SHORT STORY FOUND ON ONLINE FORUM – TIED TO HAUNTING FAMILY AFTER DEATH OF GRANDPARENT.

DRAWINGS FROM MULTIPLE DECADES BY CHILDREN – SIMILARITIES TO EACH OTHER AND STRANGER

MATCHES WHAT I SAW

SEE ON STRANGER WALK

WHAT IS HE HALLUCINATING?

SOURCE THIS

ieorge Davies
:e: Callous Heart Sketches
o: Lilly Banning

GD

i Lilly,

/anted to give you a little breathing space after our previous email. How are things moving
n? Are you holding up? I understand the toll a personal case can take, and do hope you
ıanaged to take a step back from the files.

ieorge

ect: Re:

ne here. You were right - I moved straight on to The Stranger files upon your reply.

ıd out what happened to th

Lilly,

anted to give you a little breathing space after our previous email. How are things moving on? Are you holding up?
nderstand the toll a personal case can take, and do hope you managed to take a step back from the files.

orge

ne here. You were right - I moved straight on to The Stranger files upon your reply.

nd out what happened to him.

i Lilly,

/anted to give you a little breathing space after our previous email. How are things moving on? Are you holding up?
understand the toll a personal case can take, and do hope you managed to take a step back from the files.

eorge

SOUTH COAST

DEMONOLOGY

BY GEORGE DENBROUGH

Within the sullen walls of the Bargate lurketh one of the most ardent and weather worn tales of Southampton: the tale of the "Stranger".

Mentions of a "robed watcher", "strange voyeur" and "A black mass, seen o'er her bed" can be found in documents and etchings dating back as far as the sackings of the city by the pirate Grimaldi.

In fact, many believe that the Ghoul, whose cloaked, masked form appears only to those in states of woe of distress, travelled to the southern British Isle shores aboard Grimaldi's damned fleet; his alien presence in Southampton's thriving merchant principality bringing forth the nomenclature of 'The Stranger'.

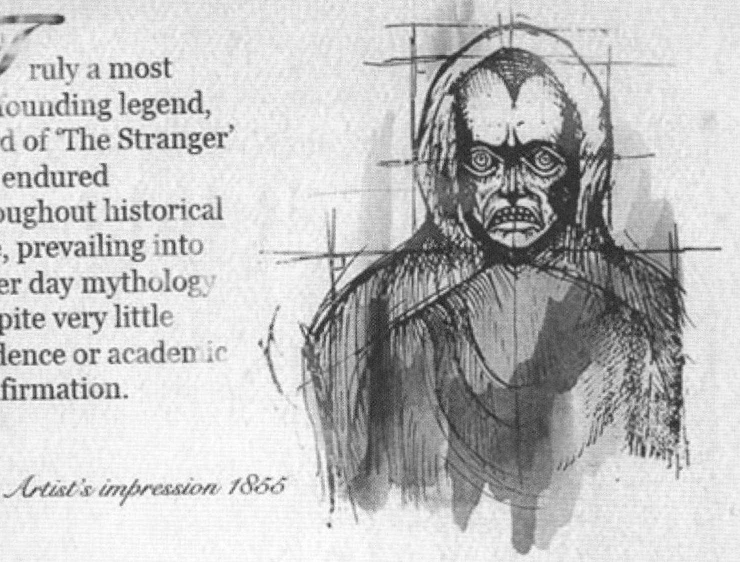

Truly a most confounding legend, word of 'The Stranger' has endured throughout historical lore, prevailing into latter day mythology despite very little evidence or academic confirmation.

Artist's impression 1855

The most numerate instances of bonafide reports and accounts of a cloaked figure haunting and threatening Southampton townsfolk date to the Edwardian period and the sinking of the Titanic, which Demonologists and Scholars of dark folklore attribute to the substantial fog of grief which shrouded the city at the time of that most infamous of disasters, proposing that the shared suffering and shock of the events lead to mass hallucinations, as Southampton mourned its dead so soon after recovering from the Cholera epidemics of the late 19th Century.

Sightings and so-called eyewitness of "The Stranger" place his presence in spots all across the ceremonial county, though there are higher instances of sightings around the ports, the troubled Undercroft Vault, and the Tudor

HISTORY OF
SOUTHAMPTON
A LOOK AT THE 2000 YEAR HISTORY OF SOUTHAMPTON

SOUTHAMPTON
MYSTERIES

The Sighting at
BEDFORD PLACE
By Edward Wayne

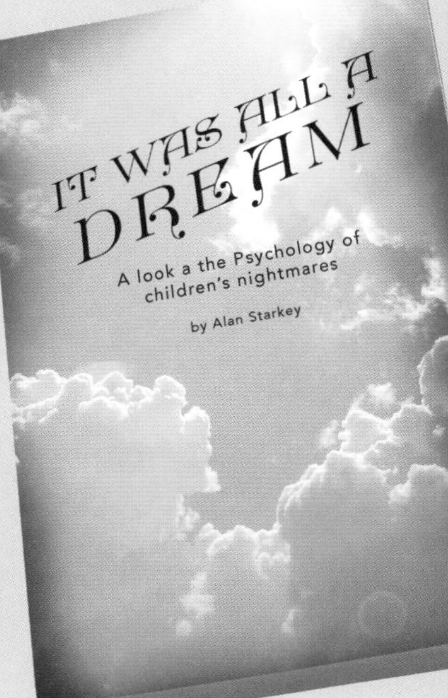

IT WAS ALL A
DREAM
A look a the Psychology of
children's nightmares
by Alan Starkey

SOUTHAMPTON
PUBLIC LIBRARY

JAMES SCYTHE

EXPIRES 26/12

STN

24. JUL 08
12 SEP 2008
07. OCT 08
29. OCT 08
M.Blair
27. NOV 08
30. DEC 08
11. APR 09
20. MAY 09
P.Smith
10. JUN 09
24. JUN 09

16. JUL 09
31. JUL 09
15. SEP 12
C.Falls
29. SEP 12
S.Butch
02. DEC 12
24. DEC 15
J.SCYTHE
4. MAY 17
L.BANNING

A/F

Please return on or before the due date.
You can renew on-line at
http://library.southampton.gov.uk
or by phone 023 8083 2597

Southampton City Council - Libraries

SOTON TIMES

PROPERTY OF OTP

No. 2722. 22 FEBRUARY 1850.—PUBLISHED EVERY TUESDAY AND FRIDAY MORNING.

ONE OF THE OLDEST REPORTS I CAN FIND DATES TO 1850, WHERE SOTON RESIDENT MICHAEL BERNARD REPORTED AN INTRUDER TO HIS HOME IN SHIRLEY ON FEBUARY 18TH. HIS REPORT READ:

I WOKE TO FIND MY WHOLE BODY PARALYSED, IT WAS AS IF SOMEONE HAD CAST A SPELL OVER ME. AS I LAY THERE IN ABJECT TERROR, I NOTICED A TALL BLACK FIGURE IN MY HALLWAY. HE WAS UNUSUALLY TALL, SO MUCH SO THAT AS HE SLOWLY ENTERED MY BEDROOM HE HAD TO DUCK TO GET UNDERNEATH THE DOOR FRAME. HE DIDNT SAY A WORD, HE JUST STOOD THERE STARING AT ME. HIS FACE WAS EGGSHELL WHITE WITH THIS HORRIBLE PURPLE MOUTH, LIKE NOTHING IVE EVER SEEN.

JAMES SEEMS TO HAVE SOURCED COPIES OF THE DOCUMENTS LISTED ON STRANGE SOUTHAMPTON

Welcome, visitor

You have to register before you can post to our site

SECRET TRUTHS. THE OTHER SIDE. YOUR FUTURE.
THE OCCULT. LIFE AFTER DEATH. THE LIVING DEAD.

SOOTHSAYER MAGAZINE

FEATURING:

YOUR WEEKLY UPDATE FROM MADAME DARLING

CAN YOU VISIT YOUR OWN GRAVE?

THE OCCULT: THE CANCER CURE

PROBING THE FLYING SAUCER RIDDLE

My story

osted by Anonymous ¦ 11.4.03 23:55 ¦ 21 comments

o I'm not sure if this is the right forum to post this under but as people keep asking me to share it, here's my ory.

was 16 years old in July 1997, still in school and still living with my parents in Southampton.
y grandmother had recently moved in with us too, so my parents had set her up a bedroom in our study.
oved my grandmother very much but she had been battling stomach cancer for a number of years and her ondition was getting worse and worse.

he stress of seeing her condition deteriorate even began to affect my studies.
would frequently come home to find Mum crying in the kitchen, as if she'd began mourning the loss of her other even prior to her death.
hink in the back of my mind I'd always assumed that Grandma would pull though, I remember even feeling nnoyed with my Mum for being so defeatist.
he thing is you have no real concept of death at 16 and in all honestly it's still impossible for me to take on oard now.

don't remember what I was doing when my father called me into the living room on the morning of Grandmas eath, but I do remember knowing immediately what had happened.
here was a tangible sadness in the room.
y mother leaked and spilled her despair from the corner as my father tried to explain.
othing was really ever the same after that; I guess nothing can prepare you to bury someone so close.

he mourning lasted weeks, we all cried together but my mother cried the hardest. I'll never forget how hard er heart was broken.
t night I would her sobbing through the wall of my bedroom, trying to conceal and silence her grief as not to ake my father.

was around August of that year that the events begun.

started innocently enough, a banging downstairs in the night or the motion sensor on the porch light flicking n. Things we'd all mention to each other but never really worry about. But then it really began to escalate.

nce in the middle of the night my mother and father woke me up, furious that I had played a prank on them. hey claimed I had thrown their bedroom door open and that it banged the wall so hard they both shot out of ed.
ried to explain it wasn't me, they refused to believe me.

nother time my mother shot up in bed next to my father screaming claiming someone had whispered her ame into her ear.
fter this she stopped reporting these instances to us both and there was a noticeable change in her.

he became quiet and seemed almost repressed.
the mornings at breakfast she would not say a word to Dad and I.
would ask my Dad about it and he would always say
'our mother is dealing with a lot right now".

hen one night, I realised why.

awoke suddenly in the night, in my bed.
here was no bang to wake me up, there was no light springing on, I just suddenly awoke.
immediately realised that I couldn't move. My body was stuck still in the bed, I couldn't even raise my hand my face.
o I had no choice but to lay there just staring around my room.
uddenly I noticed something so terrifying that it feels like it will be ingrained in me forever.
he bedroom door very slowly opened, I lay there paralysed, staring.
Vhat happened next is going to make me sound crazy but I swear to god it's true.

black-cloaked figure crept into my bedroom.

must have been 7ft tall, honestly it had to duck to get under the doorframe.
moved slowly and with absolute confidence.
iradually it lifted its head to reveal a demonic white face.
was absolutely terrified.

Seeing an actual demon in such a regular surrounding like my teenage bedroom is something I'll never forge
Then just as it crept to the foot of my bed, I woke up and it was morning.
It was bizarre, as if no time had passed at all.

I could move again but was absolutely shaken to my core as I heard my Dad call me downstairs for breakfas
When I got into the kitchen my mother was sat there in silence staring forward, like she had been doing for th
last few weeks.
I sat next to her, also in complete silence.

My Dad rushed off to work leaving my mother and I to eat breakfast in silence together.
As soon as he'd closed the front door though, my Mother turned her head towards me, slowly the way an ow
and through a terrified mouth asked
"Have you seen it too?".

I won't bore you with exact details of what happened in the years after this but I will try to summarise.
Our whole family sought counselling which was really helpful for us.
We learnt that what we were seeing was most probably our brains trying to digest the trauma and grief it had
just been through.
We'd allowed it to manifest itself into a haunting of sorts, apparently this can be quite common.

We managed to get through a lot of those hard time together, and thankfully Mum is doing a lot better now as
am I.

I will never forget what it was like to be that terrified though.
Nothing will ever change how real it felt.

Comments include :
"Thank you for sharing your story"
"May you find peace through your grief"
"I too have experienced this, but didn't receive similar support.
I wonder how differently things would have been if we had experienced this together."

SOOTHY SPOTS. CAN YOU HELP?

We've received a letter from Mrs Julia Benton who was staying with a friend in Southampton across the Summer. She says on the evening of July 31st 1962, having seen an old friend who reminded her of a painful past earlier that day, she was frightened by the appearance of a figure in her room.

"So I'm in a sleeping bag on the sofa, just about to drift off to sleep when for some reason I glance toward the window. It's then I see him, his face behind the blind. He's staring straight at me. Familiar, yet terrifying. Suddenly my entire body is unable to move.

"He must be seven foot tall, he's huge. He did nothing, just stared with this mask. On one hand, I'm terrified, one the other I'm comforted by the familiarity. I swore it would be Dennis – we didn't part ways too well, but he as alibis and proof. It was busy outside and no one saw anyone fitting the descrip-tion, or height. What could be the explanation? Could it be something supernatural?"

Well, Julia. I can't speak for Dennis' alibis but this does sound something otherworldly. Who said it was a he? As far as we can tell this is just a large being – classic spirit. We're glad you reached out to us, and we're more than happy to help. For anyone in a similar situation to Julia, please get in touch with information of your mystery and a cheque for £49.99 FAO Soothsayer Sleuthing, at the same address as usual. We'll get our people on the case.

As for Dennis, forget about him. I can see his future is cloudy, and you're better off without his influence in your life. If you'd like to know specifics of your life with and without Dennis, or any other people, please get in touch with your bank details to Soothsayer Readings, and we can put your mind at ease.

SECRET

THIS IS A COVER SHEET FOR CLASSIFIED INFORMATION

ALL INDIVIDUALS HANDLING THIS INFORMATION ARE REQUIRED TO PROTECT IT FROM UNAUTHORISED DISCLOSURE IN THE INTEREST OF NATIONAL SECURITY UNDER THE SECRET ORDER OF THE NATURAL.

HANDLING, STORAGE, REPRODUCTION AND DISPOSITION OF THE ATTACHED DOCUMENT MUST BE IN APPLICABLE EXECUTIVE ORDER(S), STATUTE(S) AND AGENCY IMPLEMENTING REGULATIONS.

INDIVIDUALS HANDLING THIS INFORMATION ARE REQUIRED TO HAVE RECEIVED THE RELEVANT LEVEL OF CLEARANCE.

RESTRICTED DATA

THE ATTACHED DOCUMENT CONTAINS RESTRICTED DATA AS DEFINED IN THE PRETERNATURAL ENERGY ACT OF 1954. UNAUTHORISED DISCLOSURE SUBJECT TO ADMINISTRATIVE AND CRIMICAL SANCTIONS.

(This cover sheet is unclassified)

SECRET

903-101
EINYA 903-01-213-672

STANDARD FORM 903
Protected by SON
32 OTP 2015

CONFIDENTIAL

SECRET ORDER OF THE NATURAL

[TSF1969.2098]
Order: 903

[TSF1969.2098]

Agent J infiltrated the group, dubbed 'the true believers' colloquially in ████████. J, name ████████, is the organisation's most trusted agent, and he proposed a distinctive link between the group and the subject. Years after the event, ████████ the fear is explained. Granters remained elusive. collectively grieving,

CONFIDENTIAL

SECRET ORDER OF THE NATURAL

[TSF1972.1087]
Order: 939

.1972.1087]

: J ██████ was invited for interview to discuss the work-based trauma he
ars to be suffering. During this process he was made to sign a non-disclosure
ement based on his 1967 case and his increasingly erratic behaviour. While J has
ys maintained utmost respect for the secrecy of the agency, he is now a risk. Tran-
ot below.
rview between J - ██████ - and Agent ██████.

I'm sorry to have to do this, ██████. But we've had reports that you've been
ning out beyond your remit and telling people of the ██████ 1967.

know I shouldn't have, but you don't understand. The ██████ exists, you just
to believe. The fear was irresponsible, an irrational reaction to what they don't
rstand. Those who understand grief, they see it.

You're a professional, ██████. We can't have you breaking strict codes put in
e for the security of our nation. You understand that, yes?

do, but-

And you understand we need you to sign this non-disclosure prohibiting you from
issing this ever again. We can't have people wondering about this kind of thing,
her you believe it to be true or not, it needs to be quashed.

ook at me, ██████. We've worked together for decades. You trust me. That's why I
assigned to the ██████. Why do you doubt me now?

We understand that you've had a hard time these last few years, the loss of-
hat's got nothing to do with this and you know it. If anything, it makes me see
rer.

Distress can manifest in many ways, and take a long time to show. The bosses think
re becoming a liability, and we need to take steps to ensure the safety of-

o you think I'm a liability?

That is irrelevant.

hey're called the believers for a reason, you know.

Let me guess, they believe in what you do?

hey understand. They've known loss that you will never understand. They've seen
██████
██████. Take ██████, she
██████. The purest of belief in

RESTRICTED DATA
This document contains restricted data as defined in the Preternatural Energy Act of 1954. Its transmittal or the disclosure of its contents in any manner to an unauthorised person is prohibited.

CONFIDENTIAL

CONFIDENTIAL

SECRET ORDER OF THE NATURAL

[TSF1972.1087]

Order: 939

something greater means ████████████████ chance to see a better future. Time and again.

██ - Do you hear yourself, ████? Do you see what you're asking people to believe?

J - If you believe then you don't know what's possible. The world is made of faith, and trust-

██ - We deal in facts. Not ████, nor ████. You may believe ████████████ but that means nothing here. I'm here as a colleague, but I'm telling you as a friend, you need to stop, for everyone's safety, particularly yours. No one can allow you to keep going like this.

J - You can silence me with your contracts, but I'll never stop believing.

██ - Your silence is all we need.

SECRET ORDER OF THE NATURAL

NON-DISCLOSURE AGREEMENT

TSF.1972.1088

Name: ████████

DOB: ████████

I, ████, agree that, in the vested interest of nation security and peace, I will:

1. Keep all information provided both to and by me in my rol ████████ in strict confidence.

2. Not make any reference to ███ case files' existence. is closed - for all intents and purposes it was never open.

3. Disclose this information to no one in perpetuity. This discussing ████████ cases with staff and governmen already aware of the periphery information.

SECRET ORDER OF THE NATURAL

TERMINATION REPORT

CASE CLOSURE

RESTRICTED DATA

This document contains restricted data as defined in the Internatural Energy Act of ... Its transmittal or the disclosure of its contents in any manner to an unauthorised person is prohibited.

[TSF1974.2987]

An investigation has been conducted by Agents ██████ and ██████ into the disappearance of Agent J, ██████. One of the most prolific within the organisation, and one of the few of such high level to warrant the code name as to offer protection in the most high level of cases.

He was last seen ████████████████████, with flags raised by ██████████ when he stopped showing up to ████████████████████████.

J signed a non-disclosure agreement on █████ 1972, five years after █████████████████, which is believed to be the case that caused his downfall. Files on this were largely destroyed by former Special Agent and CEO ████████████ who believed it to be in the interest of national security. This is one of the organisation's greatest misjustices in its history.

██

Without this, Agents ██████ and ██████ found difficulty in tracking his thoughts, and only had access to his departure interview. Agent ███████ noted that she managed to track his whereabouts the first year following his agreed silence and he simply disappeared.

Granters, of ████████████████, the only source with whom J appears to have had contact with was untraceable. He appeared to be following the same threads that were tied to ████████████████████ but there is no record, from various witnesses, of him ever breaking his NDA.

nformation remains minimal. His last noted words on record were "You can ilence me with your contracts, but I'll never stop believing", and it is eported as a note of protest, described by Agents ██████████████████████████████ and ███████████████, that he emained silent the moment he signed the contract until his departure rom the building.

RESTRICTED DATA

This document contains restricted data as defined in the Preternatural Energy Act of 1954. Its transmittal or the disclosure of its contents in any manner to an unauthorised person is prohibited.

KODAK 400TX

KODAK 400T

50

RESTRICTED DATA

This ocument contains restricted data as
de d in the Preternatural Energy Act of
954. Its transmittal or the disclosure of
s contents in any manner to an unauthor-
d person is prohibited.

SECRET

THIS IS A COVER SHEET FOR CLASSIFIED INFORMATION

ALL INDIVIDUALS HANDLING THIS INFORMATION ARE REQUIRED TO PROTECT IT FROM UNAUTHORISED DISCLOSURE IN THE INTEREST OF NATIONAL SECURITY UNDER THE SECRET ORDER OF THE NATURAL.

HANDLING, STORAGE, REPRODUCTION AND DISPOSITION OF THE ATTACHED DOCUMENT MUST BE IN APPLICABLE EXECUTIVE ORDER(S), STATUTE(S) AND AGENCY IMPLEMENTING REGULATIONS.

INDIVIDUALS HANDLING THIS INFORMATION ARE REQUIRED TO HAVE RECEIVED THE RELEVANT LEVEL OF CLEARANCE.

RESTRICTED DATA

THIS DOCUMENT CONTAINS RESTRICTED DATA AS DEFINED IN THE PRETERNATURAL ENERGY ACT OF 1954. ITS TRANSMITTAL OR THE DISCLOSURE OF ITS CONTENTS IN ANY MANNER TO AN UNAUTHORISED PERSON IS PROHIBITED.

(This cover sheet is unclassified)

SECRET

903-101
EINYA 903-01-213-672

STANDARD FORM 903
Protected by SON
32 OTP 2015

63% 09:23

Louise
+447931021214

Friday, 8 May, 2017

Hey, Louise, sorry to bother you so late and out of work! Quick Q, who would have access in the office to restricted files? Ones from 40-50 years ago? It's Lilly btw, not sure if I have you my number.
00:13

Hey! I didn't have it so thanks. The highest level George has access to is top secret. Restricted is a few above that so no one in the office has access. If you need something for the case there might be someone higher up to talk to but I don't remember ever seeing anything in the office above TS an

VIEW ALL
00:15

Don't need anything, thanks though. Hypothetically if someone did get a restricted file in our office how would they do that?
00:16

Are you planning something? ;) jk. Honestly those files are locked. No legal way to get hold of them. Im 99.9% sure no one has put in requests, at least not in my time, but I can double check for you tomorrow. but even

few above that so no one in the office has access. If you need something for the case there might be someone higher up to talk to but I don't remember ever seeing anything in the office above TS an

VIEW ALL
00:15

Don't need anything, thanks though. Hypothetically if someone did get a restricted file in our office how would they do that?
00:16

Are you planning something? ;) jk. Honestly those files are locked. No legal way to get hold of them. Im 99.9% sure no one has put in requests, at least not in my time, but I can double check for you tomorrow. but even through the right means those files never usually see the light of day once they'

VIEW ALL
00:18

That makes sense. If you could check that would be perfect. I don't keep you any longer, enjoy the rest of your evening out! Hope the drinks are flowing
00:19

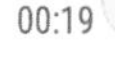

Hey, as suspected no restricted file has been through this office in decades. Not sure I can do much more digging for you without it looking suspicious so hope that answers what you need?
09:20

Enter message

SEND

PROPERTY OF OTP

17TH NOVEMBER 2015

I DON'T KNOW WHO TO TELL SO I'M LEFT WITH THE PAGE. THIS... PERSON? BEING? WAS LURKING OUTSIDE MY HOME, CAME IN MY HOME... TALL, CLOAKED, MASKED. JUST STOOD THERE. IT FEELS LIKE THE HORRORS I'VE BEEN READING ABOUT. TODAY HAS BEEN ROUGH, IT'S BEEN NINE YEARS SINCE MARY. I KNOW MOST OF THAT I WAS HIDING AWAY IN MY HAPPIER PASTS AND PRETENDING I WAS A CAREFREE CHILD AGAIN, BUT IT'S ALWAYS STUNG.

WHO IS THIS? THEY FELT FAMILIAR. I FELT LIKE I KNEW THEM. I FELT THE SAME AS I HAD THOSE YEARS OF SAFETY AT HOME. BUT I WAS TERRIFIED TOO. I WAS LYING ON THE FLOOR, UNABLE TO MOVE. CONFLICTED. HOW IS IT POSSIBLE TO FEEL BOTH AT ONCE?

I FEEL LIKE A FRAUD. I RESEARCH ALL THESE MYTHS AND LEGENDS THAT I BELIEVED, AND WHEN ONE IS STARING ME IN THE FACE, THEN DOUBT DECIDES TO STRIKE. DO I REALLY BELIEVE? OR DO I WANT TO? IS THERE A DIFFERENCE? AM I READY TO LET GO AND FULLY SUBMERGE MYSELF IN THESE WORLDS? MARY ALWAYS FOUND MYTHS A CURIOSITY AND MY FASCINATION WITH THEM MORE SO. IF SHE WERE HERE, NONE OF THIS WOULD BE HAPPENING... WHO KNOWS WHERE WE'D BE...

Gi Group

MEETING WITH ELLA STARKEY, DESCENDENT OF ALAN STARKEY, AUTHOR OF IT WAS ALL A DREAM, MAY 2017

LB: Thank you for talking to me, I realise it's a bit of an odd query.
ES: Not a problem. It's not too odd considering my grandfather's book, but I understand your point.

LB: Do you know why your grandfather decided to write his book, and include drawings and patient's files?
ES: Ultimately Alan was a good man, and he really loved his work. I think if you look at the actual content of what he writes on child psychology in It Was All A Dream, it's important work, and it demystifies a lot of the subject matter for people who might be unaware and looking to understand the psychology of themselves, others around them or the topic in general. I disagree with his inclusion of specifics and documents.

LB: He sought their permission though?
ES: I'm led to believe so – that's what he said. I know some people whose drawings from childhood are in the book say they didn't give their permission, but it gets complicated – they were children, their parents might have granted permission, it's a murky area.

LB: As these stories are in the public domain, I wondered if I could ask you about one particular section?
ES: You can ask, but I need to underline patient confidentiality here. I won't breach that at all, so if there's any risk of that I apologise in advance if my answers aren't of use to you.

LB: I don't know if you've seen the Strange Southampton website-
ES: Ugh, I have heard of it. Are you going to waste my time with some random guy's ramblings?

LB: No, it's not that. I first came across your grandfather's book through some drawings they had on the website. The Stranger – I'm not sure that these are attributed to The Stranger in his book, but they all seem to be of the same cloaked figure.
ES: There are many cloaked figures – death, for one. Characters in folklore, in popular culture. And yes, I guess, "The Stranger".

LB: Doesn't it seem strange that so many children were drawing the same figure following a loss? The book covers a number of cases in a short space but the further research people have undertaken has shown hundreds, thousands of similar cases.
ES: Does it seem strange that following death and grief children appear to be drawing a grim reaper type figure? No, I don't think so.

LB: But it goes beyond that – the faces are the same, give or take the drawing and decade it's from. The indentations or marks on the face are all the same. It does seem like something more specific than a general notion of death. And your grandfather's book discloses that the descriptions of height match up, setting – The Stranger shows up in their homes, walks into their lives – they share similar feelings – a mix of terror and comfort at some kind of familiarity. The links go deeper than being a grim reaper type figure. Has anyone more recently spoke about this? Surely it still continues.
ES: You must know I couldn't answer a question like that. If that had been the case it would not be my place to talk about it on behalf of any of my patients. I appreciate you want to talk to me about this above others in the field for obvious reasons, but I am not my grandfather – I don't entertain the

notions he does. I am a woman of science.

LB: Do you believe that The Stranger exists? I know you can't talk about it, but I believe that you, above all others, are who people would come to now, given your heritage. You must have seen dozens, hundreds of cases over the years perhaps. Do you believe it could exist?
ES: Do I believe it could exist? I believe people might think it exists to get through difficult times. The more this legend grows, the more comfort can be drawn from it, despite the terror this being also inspires. As I said, I'm a woman of science, and I'm here to help people, not speculate.

LB: It could be more than a comforting idea-
ES: Let me ask you, Ms. Banning. Do you believe The Stranger exists?

LB: I didn't. For a long time, I didn't. I'm not so sure now. My friend, he was looking into this and he went missing and I just...
ES: If you don't mind me saying, I feel like you're wanting to hear me say I believe in The Stranger to bring strength to feelings you're currently navigating. If you're unsure on its existence, you need the validation to really commit. As I said, I fully believe this being exists in people's minds and has done for decades as a comfort in dark times, and if your friend has gone missing then the idea of this mythical being bringing comfort in dark times is something to cling to. It's something to consider.

LB: It goes back decades, centuries – beyond my lifetime. I can't see how-
ES: Ms. Banning, I can't help you on this. I really can't. I'm sorry but I must get back to work.

Section of drawings taken from Alan Starkey's seminal exploration in text, It Was All A Dream. Individuals have not been identified to follow up with, but their experiences – as outlined in the book – align. They were constricted with fear, and felt some comfort.

"THE STRANGER"

It visited in dark periods of grief. They were torn. Their drawings all share similar characteristics beyond being cloaked, leading to the determination that it was the same being in question.

WORLD'S FAIR 1967

NEW SECTION ON SITE, COULD HOLD CLUES.
WORLD FAIRS: STARTED 1800S, COMING TOGETHER OF
NATIONS TO SHARE THEIR IDEAS AND HOPES FOR THE FUTURE.
CHECK WIKI LINK
MOST FAMOUS 1964-65 IN NEW YORK – THOROUGHLY
DOCUMENTED. LOOK INTO NY – PARALLELS TO SOUTHAMPTON?
HISTORY – WW2 HIT SOUTHAMPTON HARD. 1950S – CITY
BEGUN TO PICK ITSELF UP / REBUILD. DECIDED TO
CELEBRATE COMING TOGETHER OF ADVANCES OF TECH
FROM ALL OVER WORLD BY HOSTING WORLDS FAIR THERE
FAIR – THEME: COLLABORATION. AIM: 'SHAKE HANDS WITH THE
STRANGER OF TOMORROW'. 6 PAVILIONS: DREAM, SPACE, TRIUMPH
OF MAN, BRITISH DEVELOPMENT, SOUTHAMPTON, TWO
CYLINDRICAL TOWERS. (TICKETING AND SOUVENIRS TOO)
VIDEO – ABANDONED SOUTHAMPTON. GENERAL FACTS ON
CITY. FAIR: DESIGNED TO PUT AWAY FEARS FROM WAR AND
LOOK TO FUTURE. OPEN ARMS, OPEN MIND. ALMOST ALL
SITE NOW DEVELOPED ON (50 YEARS ON), INCLUDING ST
MARYS STADIUM (OPEN 2001). CYLINDRICAL TOWERS STILL
THERE – MIRRORS NY. STRANGE RUMOURS OF WHAT HAPPENED
AT FAIR, SKETCHY REPORTS OF MASS DISRUPTION. SOMEONE
TRYING TO DERAIL THE FAIR. UNLIKE TODAY – NO
SMARTPHONES, SO NO VIDEO PROOF. 50TH ANNIVERSARY CELEBRATION?
MORE LIGHT SHED ON MYSTERIES?

????

FIND PEOPLE INVOVLED

ECHO DAILY COVERAGE – 'STRANGE HAPPENINGS AT THE
WORLD'S FAIR' 'REPORTS OF DISRUPTION' 'YOU HAVE
NOTHING TO FEAR' SAYS FAIR ADMINISTRATORS – FULL
ARTICLE?

SHAKE HANDS WITH
THE STRANGER OF TOMORROW
World's Fair 1967

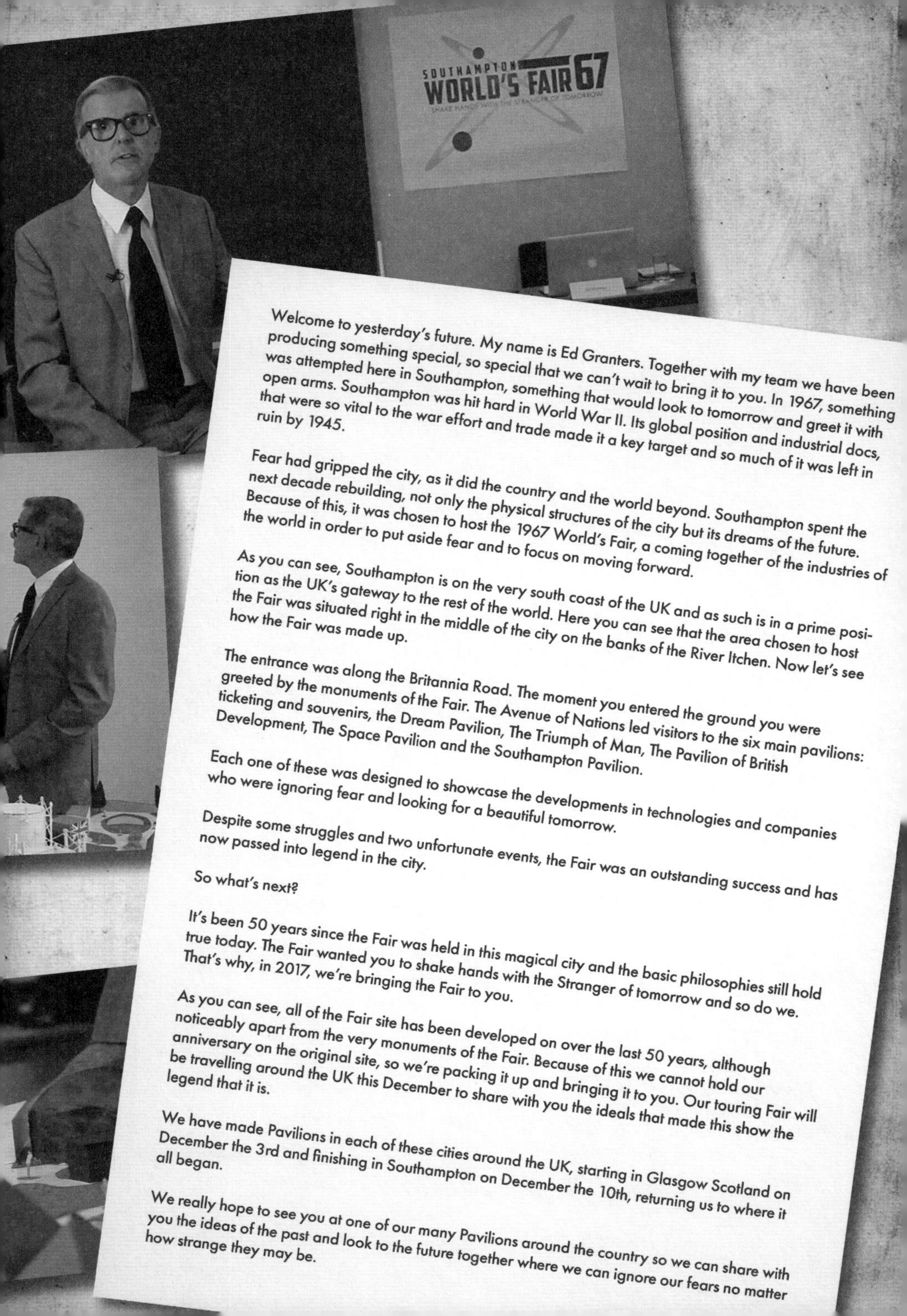
SOUTHAMPTON
WORLD'S FAIR 67
SHAKE HANDS WITH THE STRANGER OF TOMORROW

Welcome to yesterday's future. My name is Ed Granters. Together with my team we have been producing something special, so special that we can't wait to bring it to you. In 1967, something was attempted here in Southampton, something that would look to tomorrow and greet it with open arms. Southampton was hit hard in World War II. Its global position and industrial docs, that were so vital to the war effort and trade made it a key target and so much of it was left in ruin by 1945.

Fear had gripped the city, as it did the country and the world beyond. Southampton spent the next decade rebuilding, not only the physical structures of the city but its dreams of the future. Because of this, it was chosen to host the 1967 World's Fair, a coming together of the industries of the world in order to put aside fear and to focus on moving forward.

As you can see, Southampton is on the very south coast of the UK and as such is in a prime position as the UK's gateway to the rest of the world. Here you can see that the area chosen to host the Fair was situated right in the middle of the city on the banks of the River Itchen. Now let's see how the Fair was made up.

The entrance was along the Britannia Road. The moment you entered the ground you were greeted by the monuments of the Fair. The Avenue of Nations led visitors to the six main pavilions: ticketing and souvenirs, the Dream Pavilion, The Triumph of Man, The Pavilion of British Development, The Space Pavilion and the Southampton Pavilion.

Each one of these was designed to showcase the developments in technologies and companies who were ignoring fear and looking for a beautiful tomorrow.

Despite some struggles and two unfortunate events, the Fair was an outstanding success and has now passed into legend in the city.

So what's next?

It's been 50 years since the Fair was held in this magical city and the basic philosophies still hold true today. The Fair wanted you to shake hands with the Stranger of tomorrow and so do we. That's why, in 2017, we're bringing the Fair to you.

As you can see, all of the Fair site has been developed on over the last 50 years, although noticeably apart from the very monuments of the Fair. Because of this we cannot hold our anniversary on the original site, so we're packing it up and bringing it to you. Our touring Fair will be travelling around the UK this December to share with you the ideals that made this show the legend that it is.

We have made Pavilions in each of these cities around the UK, starting in Glasgow Scotland on December the 3rd and finishing in Southampton on December the 10th, returning us to where it all began.

We really hope to see you at one of our many Pavilions around the country so we can share with you the ideas of the past and look to the future together where we can ignore our fears no matter how strange they may be.

Evening Standard

44,201 THURSDAY, NOVEMBER 3, 1966 4d.

WELCOME TO THE WORLD

Southampton has been named the next city to host the renowned World's Fair next year, in 1967. The city follows in the grand footsteps of Paris, Chicago and New York in hosting the iconic celebration.

Southampton will be sharing the honour in 1967 with Montreal, who are yet to reveal the theme of their celebration. For those who regularly travel to World's Fairs, it has been confirmed that while the dates are yet to be announced, there will be several months between the two Fairs.

Buzz is building around the landmarks for the Fair – Montreal has been developing a 'Biosphere' with R. Buckminster Fuller in anticipation of receiving this honour. Southampton, following its development post-war, did not go down this route and instead relied on the city's drive and spirit to win the bid.

Landmarks of note from previous Fairs include the Eiffel Tower in Paris and the Golden Gate Bridge, both of which were tied greatly to their event in 1889 and 1939 respectively. The question now for Southampton is: where? What landmark of our fine city will join these illustrio ranks? With developm the Fair site to begin imminently, we shoulc soon.

The World's Fair comr are currently welcomi suggestions for theme taglines of the Fair a be hosting an open f Central Hall (St Mary 7PM on Monday 7.

GAIETY
OPEN DAILY
2 P.M. until 10.45 P.M.
PICTURES
'Truth About Wives'

SAYBURN'S
SAYONA
RADIOLA Service
Radio Repairs
RADIOLA Service
WORLD'S FAIR 67
SAYBURN'S

Photos from Southampton around World's Fair weekend.
Specific date, time and photographer unknown

The Echo Daily

STRANGE HAPPENINGS AT THE WORLD'S FAIR

REPORTS OF DISRUPTION AT CITY'S ATTRACTION

You have nothing to fear" say the air's administrators

HE ICONIC World's Fair celebrations were with 'chaos' this weekend in its host city of uthampton. Reports have been circulating that ass panic was caused causing a crowd surge not ng after 3pm on Saturday afternoon. Screams portedly echoed around the Dream Pavilion, ough accounts do differ on the exact location. is caused a knock-on effect with panic spread-. Various attendees noted the owing: "There we were, chatting to some ows from Montreal – said they'd had a lovely e at their Fair – and bang. We heard what we ught was fireworks in the middle of the day. no, it would have to be a gun at this time. ste of fireworks. We ran. [...] Yes, I suppose it could have just been something dropped. [...] Yes, but it was scary nonetheless."

"I was hit with a wave of panic. Everything blurred, but there was a dark figure standing in the middle of it all. Perfectly still. I couldn't see their face, but I haven't felt like that since the accident a few years ago."

"Everyone was running towards me, and so I ran with the tide. Otherwise I would be trampled. I don't know what caused it, but I knew I wasn't going to stand there."

The panic was calmed within approximately thirty minutes and the source cannot be verified. Founder Mr. Granters spoke to the Echo following the Fair noting: "The World's Fair in Southampton was an unequivocal success. A real testament to the spirit and spark of the people of the city, and the sort of level we can play on the World stage."

When pressed on the incident, Granters continued: "Events of this scale rarely go off without a hitch. We are pleased to have been able to welcome thousands from world-over and have them join us to look to the future and shake hands with the stranger of tomorrow."

The World's Fair is the highest attended event in Southampton's history, with over 135,000 people entering the gates across the three days.

1 2 3

A

SOUTHAMPTON WORLD'S FAIR 67

SHAKE HANDS WITH THE STRANGER OF TOMORROW

B

OFFICIAL SOUVENIR MAP

C

D

E

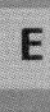

F

G

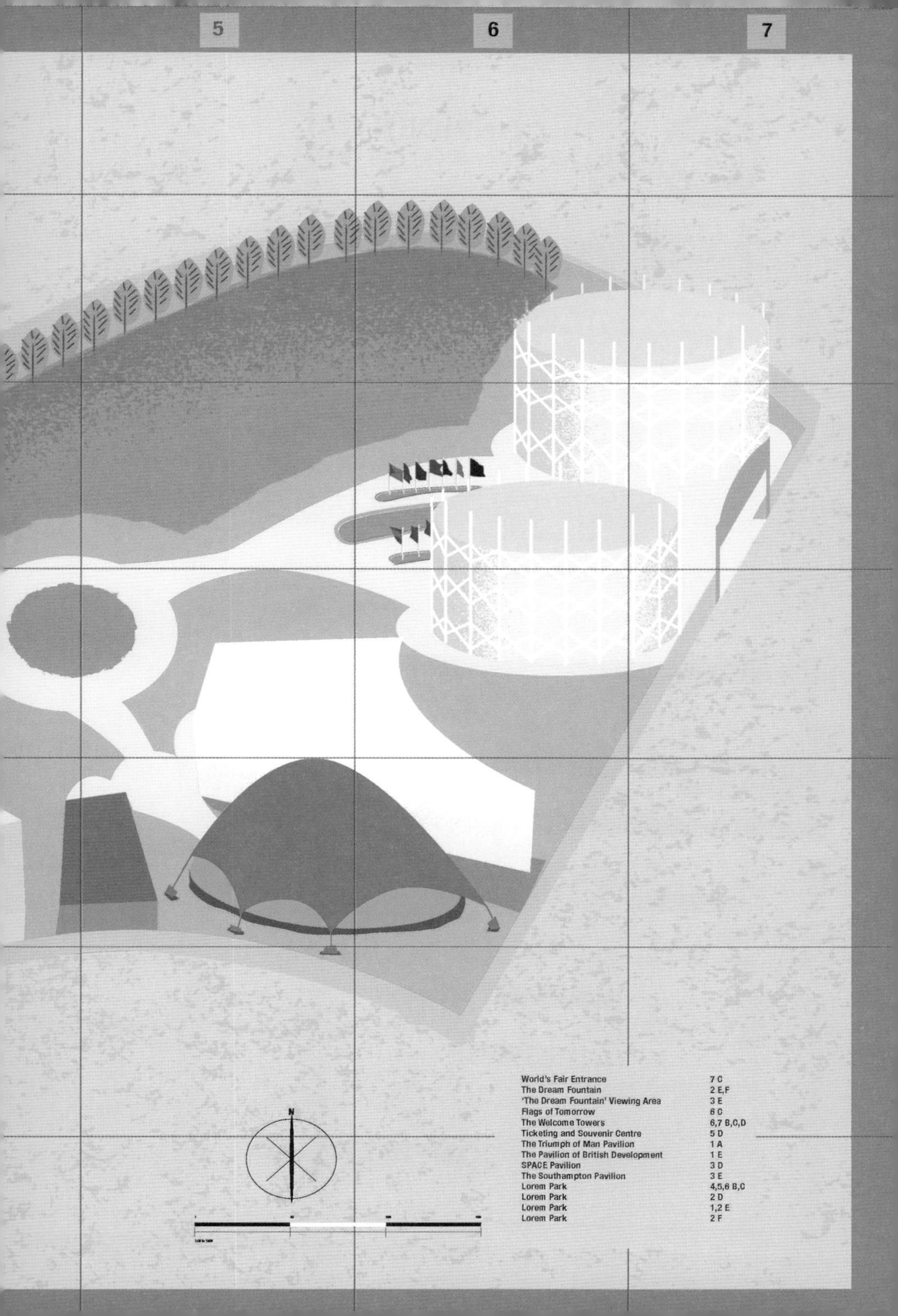
5
6
7
N
World's Fair Entrance 7 C
The Dream Fountain 2 E,F
'The Dream Fountain' Viewing Area 3 E
Flags of Tomorrow 6 C
The Welcome Towers 6,7 B,C,D
Ticketing and Souvenir Centre 5 D
The Triumph of Man Pavilion 1 A
The Pavilion of British Development 1 E
SPACE Pavilion 3 D
The Southampton Pavilion 3 E
Lorem Park 4,5,6 B,C
Lorem Park 2 D
Lorem Park 1,2 E
Lorem Park 2 F

CONFIDENTIAL

SECRET ORDER OF THE NATURAL

[TSF1977.2917]
Order: 1033

TWFF.1977.2917

Interview conducted on 31.12.75 by Agent . Interviewee Mr. Edward Joseph Granters, founder of the World's Fair Southampton. Following reports of strange incidents at the Fair in 1967, Granters was unable to be traced. The only reported comments in public domain were a pre-prepared statement submitted to multiple newspaper sources on the Fair's success, and one direct reply to a query on the incidents that unfolded.

He was located on 29.12.75, over eight years after the Fair and immediately brought in for questioning. The conversation is contained below.

: Mr. Granters, thank you for your patience in getting this arranged. It's an odd time of year, but you understand we couldn't risk you disappearing again.
EG: Of course. I do understand that.

: Would you care to explain where you disappeared to following the Fair in 1967?
EG: I treated myself to a holiday and decided to travel the world. Is that a crime? It seems so from the way you are acting.

: You have to understand that after what happened at the Fair people would want to talk to you.
EG: A minor scuffle? A wave of panic? Seems nothing to me.

: It seems quite a coincidence considering the theme of the Fair that reports suggest .
EG: Hearsay.

: Hardly hearsay, Mr. Granters. A colleague of ours, , was investigating the occurrences at your Fair and he drew quite a lot of conclusions. , for one. We've been unable to locate him
EG: Not very good at locating people, evidently. Do you believe him? Do you really thin ?

: I'm not here to answer questions. If people had listened to sooner than people might have come after you sooner. It's too much of a coincidence , and then . When did you first hear of the commotion?
EG: After the Fair. I was entertaining the international delegation, the staff dealt with it. Trickle effect, people stampeding about the place. Brought under control very quickly. I still don't see why it requires the high level questioning.

: But the trigger? ? ~~He exists? It exists?~~
EG: I'd say it's all down to what you believe in. Some want to believe, some want to se what's in front of them, some want to live in denial. You can only hope when you host a event on this scale that could happen, but I most certainly did not orchestrate it, should that be what happened, though I highly doubt it is. The chances!

: Why would you hope?

RESTRICTED DATA
This document contains restricted data defined in the Preternatural Energy Act 1954. Its transmittal or the disclosure its contents in any manner to an unauthorised person is prohibited.

CONFIDENTIAL

CONFIDENTIAL

SECRET ORDER OF THE NATURAL

[TSF1977.2917]
Order: 1033

EG: Why wouldn't you? The legacy! The grandeur! On the international stage! I went away after so I could preserve the feeling of joy from the success of the Fair, not be around people who would chip away with their complaints. Oh, little Jimmy fell and hurt his knee. Oh my, the queue was too long for me. I wanted to preserve the perfection.

██: Even with ██████? So few are willing to talk about what they saw-
EG: Or they talk and you don't want to hear their story for truth.

██: Mr. Granters, will all due respect - I don't know what's going on here-
EG: Evidently.

██: What I mean by that is this is... beyond what I work with, what I consider reality. ██████? ██████? It's a big leap. But what I don't understand is why, if ██████ is indeed true, then why would you want to be part of it? Or why would you want to hide it?
EG: All I care about is the future, ██████. Maybe one day someone will experience ██████ and ██████. Perhaps. But through the fear and darkness of the world, people will look ahead and shake hands with the Stranger of tomorrow. I firmly believe in that.

██: You believe in a lot, by the sounds of it.
EG: Am I under arrest? Am I in trouble? I'm failing to see the point of any of this.

██: You'll be free to go once we're done. We're keeping you here to be thorough; I'm fine to tell you that we fully expect you'll disappear into the ether again as soon as we're done, and can't take that risk, whether we get the answers or not.
EG: That's fair. If you need a starting point, I've always thought San Antonio looked quite a good time.

RESTRICTED DATA
This document contains restricted data as defined in the Preternatural Energy Act of 1954. Its transmittal or the disclosure of its contents in any manner to an unauthorised person is prohibited.

CONFIDENTIAL

Pavilion of
BRITISH DEVELOPMENT

"Protecting you from the Ghosts of the Past"

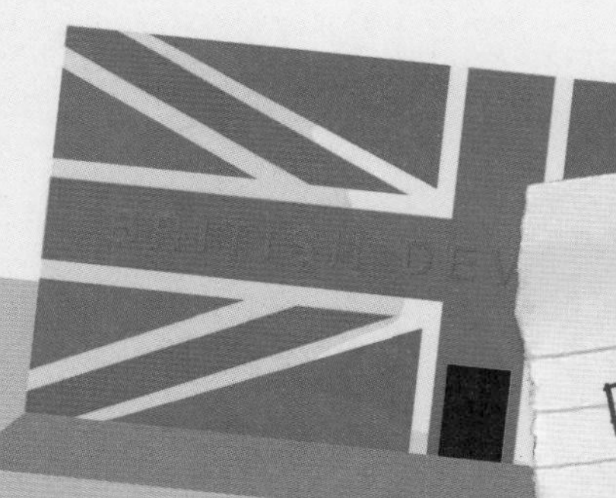

PAVILION OF BRITISH DEVELOPMENT

obviously an attempt at avoiding WWII nostalgi

a pavilion to educate new generations?

SPACE PAVILION -

"LEAVE YOUR PROBLEMS ON EARTH"

A look to the future?

Advancements of technology since the war?

SPACE PAVILION

LEAVE YOUR PROBLEMS ON EARTH

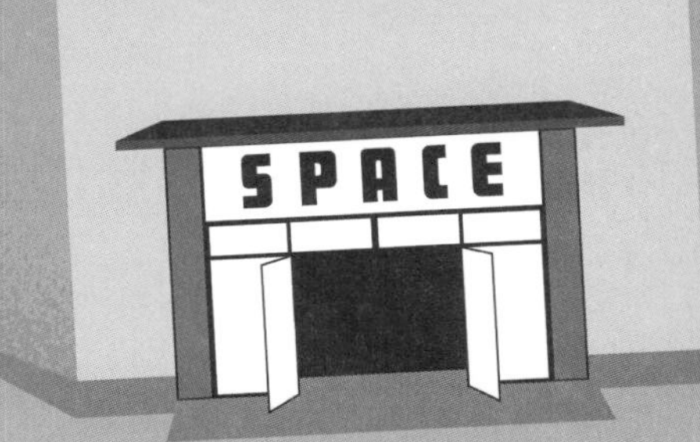

I CHECKED OUT THE SITE OF THE FAIR AND FOUND VIRTUALLY NO EVIDENCE IT EVER HAPPENED WITH THE STADIUM AND POWER GRID NOW IN ITS PLACE.

World's Fair Southampton 1967

From Wikipedia, the free encyclopedia

This article **needs additional citations for** verification. Please help improve this article by adding citations to reliable sources. Unsourced material may be challenged and removed. *(May 2009) (Learn how and when to remove this template message)*

For other World's Fair events see *The World's Fair (disambiguation)*.

The World's Fair, originating in New York City, United States of America, was similarly held in Southampton in 1967 to focus on moving forward from the continuing traumas of World War II and to 'shake hands with the stranger of tomorrow'[1]. The Fair was made up of several pavilions: ticketing and souvenirs, the Dream Pavilion, the Triumph of Man, the Pavilion of British Development, the Space Pavilion and the Southampton Pavilion.

Intended to be fun for all the family, crowds attended the first fair and it was slated to be a huge success despite some locals voicing reservations in newpapers beliving that it didn't tend of the locals of Southampton and instead sought to bring in audiences from outside and surrounding towns.[2]

Controversies sounded the fair but founder Edward Granters ignored most allegations and focused on the positive business it brought a suffering Southampton.[3]

As of 2017 there are plans to revive the fair but not in Southampton alone, it will instead be packed up and taken to a number of sites across the UK for numerous dates in December.

Contents [hide]

Map from the first 1967 World's Fair in Southampton

The now abandoned site of the original Southampton World's Fair

WIKIPEDIA
The Free Encyclopedia
Main page
Contents
Featured content
Current events
Random article
Donate to Wikipedia
Wikipedia store
Interaction
Help
About Wikipedia
Community portal
Recent changes
Contact page
Tools
What links here
Related changes
Upload file
Special pages
Permanent link
Page information
Wikidata item
Cite this page
Print/export
Create a book
Download as PDF
Printable version

Controversies [edit]

Dream Fountain – where the delegate from the USA is said to have thrown his drink after founder Granters unceremoniously (and reportedly) said, "See, my friend, this is how y
do a World's Fair."

The most likely place the 'incident' began, based on various reports, is by the Dream Pavilion. It is said to have begun with a scream, which trickled panic through the Fair and caused a stampede. Though many have claimed to have been the trigger of this, no identifiable source has been proven.[citation needed]

Several people fainted around the Welcome Towers – primarily due to heat exhaustion. They seemed to share the same hallucination of seeing a dark figure looming from the shadows, inspiring the 'hit' Halloween costume of '67 (*See also*: "The Stranger"). Police confirmed no unusual substances were in their systems.

Closure & developments [edit]

St. Mary's Stadium (home to Southampton FC) was built in 2001 over a large section of the Fair's site.

The Triumph of Ma
...how man has persevered under the cover of pro

TRIUMPH OF MAN –

"See how man has persevered under the cover of progress"
wonder if the secret egotism of Granters

DREAM PAVILION –

to fit in with the theme of forward thinking
"shake hands with the stranger of tomorrow"
dreams of a better future?

Dream Pavilion

On Saturday 17th June 2017, I held a group meeting with previous staff of the World's Fair (1967) and others who responded to my call out for information at the end of 2016. This was to discuss the original World's Fair and upcoming World's Fair tour in December 2017. After vetting of information from the callout, those invited for the full interview are:

- **Mrs. Anthea Ward (AW)** – Worked at the 1967 Fair, escorting and overseeing the schedules of international delegates.
- **Mr. Felix Whittington (FW)** – Grandson of member of staff working the Dream Pavilion in 1967.
- **Miss. Felicity Burnside (FB)** – Volunteer for World's Fair Tour 2017 committee, likely to be working the tour.
- **Mr. Angus Blair (AB)** – Staff at the original Fair. Primarily keeping the areas clean, reportedly worked near disruption.
- **Ms. Sofie Darlton (SD)** – Daughter of Ed Granters' personal assistant, David Darlton.

The group interview transcript has been moved around for legibility around specific topics. Should any notes need clarified, the full, original transcript can be supplied.

Q5. What do you remember about the "incident" that occurred at the World's Fair 1967?
AW – We had word back in the building that a commotion was occurring. Our job was to keep the delegates calm – for the majority, they were nonplussed as they were safe. They just waited for it to tide over. Afterwards, we heard the rumours about spirits and weird beings but that was completely suppressed.
SD – I know I wasn't there but my granddad used to talk about Mr. Granters really clamping down on the speculation, but he found it weird as he swore he believed in all the mythology around it.
AB – I'd say it fanned the flame more. Intriguing, ain't it? I found it gibberish. Absolute gibberish. I saw a woman scream and the ripple effect occur, saw nothing out of order, never believed any of this nonsense. But a good friend of mine, one of the smartest, brightest women I knew, swore she saw it. She travelled to the Fair from London, first real trip since the loss of Vincent. Was still pretty raw and she swears down blind that she saw the figure. Wrestled with it over the years – she never fully let herself believe it, but if she was questioning, it made me question.
LB – So you believe the rumours on it being "The Stranger"?
AB – I don't know, I honestly don't. It sounds ridiculous, but so many people saying the same thing without knowing one another, makes you wonder? If it is tied to certain life experiences, then it makes sense that only some of us would see it...?
AW – I struggle to reconcile the idea that something beyond the world was there. But I also struggle to see why you'd try so hard to suppress something that rings so clearly as fake unless there's something to it. That wouldn't have damaged the Fair.
FW – My granddad wasn't the same since the Fair. He tried to spread word of the Stranger but was clamped with legalities to stop him. That's the memory I have: he'd tell bedtime stories to me and my sister.

Q9: Will you be attending the World's Fair tour?
FB – I obviously will be. I want to maintain the legacy of the original. I don't know where the line is on the mystery around it, but I think what it stands for – the hope, the believing in the unbelievable, that's something to celebrate.
AB – I'm unsure. I like to think I could get answers but that's too much to ask. Seemingly the Granters clan are involved again and I don't think I trust them. What're they going to do, come out and say

'hey, it was all a joke' or 'hey, it's all real'? I might, I could get the answers for my friend.
FB – The son of Mr. Granters is behind the Fair, but on the brief instance I met him, he's very much into the mythology too. Wants people to experience the wonder – they'll be curious about the legacy and able to explore that too.
SD – I won't be attending. My grandad was at the original and says something funny's going on there.
FB – I swear to you nothing funny is going on.
SD – I get that, but if there is something beyond us there, then how do you know something funny won't be going on? Have you even read about the Believers? Everyone who's into that seems to be gearing up for the 50th anniversary.
AW – The Believers are an odd bunch. I know the mystique of them is their seemingly ageless quality, but I swear I saw them a decade or so after the Fair and they looked almost identical. I feel uncomfortable admitting it aloud but that alone has made me wonder, and this theory doing the rounds...

Q10: Do you think the World's Fair and its Anniversary Tour is tied to the legends of the city?
FB – Absolutely not. We're planning a great event for cities across the UK – the mystery is just a speculation.
FW – I understand you're working on the Fair so will think that, but taking a step back – when you see the impact the Fair had on people, what they saw, I find it difficult to separate the event from the rest.
AB – I don't think the Fair set out to be, but I think they're definitely tied now. I feel uneasy about the handling of it; there's something greater at play. I don't think there's a way to orchestrate the feeling of grief and passion that surrounds them but I think it would be naïve to suggest they're not secretly hoping for chaos round two.
AW – Or at least hoping to be a vessel for something. People have spent decades trying to replicate it, capture the feelings that can bring "the Stranger" and it's completely random, but if anyone can do something to show the world about the legends, proving their legitimacy or their fraudulence, then the Granters clan seem to have the world in their hands.
SD – What about you, Lilly? Do you think they're linked?
LB – I honestly don't know any more. I know someone who definitely thought they were linked, and I used to think he was falling into wormholes to cope, but now I'm not so sure. It's a tough one, isn't it?
SD – Yeah... Do you think you'll go to the Fair in December?
LB – Honestly, if I'm looking for answers, I think it would be stupid of me not to.
FB – You'll have an excellent time. Even from the blueprints, it's unlike anything I've ever seen.

THE
SOUTHAMPTON
PAVILION
"MAKE A STRANGER YOUR NEW BEST FRIEND"

THE SOUTHAMPTON PAVILION

Obvious celebration of the host city –
Montreal had a similarly named pavilion as a centre piece to theirs.

SOUTHAMPTON

WORLD'S FAIR 67

SHAKE HANDS WITH THE STRANGER OF TOMORROW

50 YEARS AGO WE ALL GOT TOGETHER TO MEET THE STRANGER OF TOMORROW. NOW HE'S COMING TO YOU.

50TH ANNIVERSARY TOUR
DECEMBER 2017

03 THE GLASGOW PAVILION
04 THE BIRMINGHAM PAVILION
07 THE LONDON PAVILION
09 THE MANCHESTER PAVILION
10 THE SOUTHAMPTON PAVILIO

TRANSCRIPT WITH ED GRANTERS JR., SON OF ED GRANTERS, THE FOUNDER OF THE WORLD'S FAIR. JULY, 2015.

JS: Thank you again for talking to me Mr. Granters, you're a difficult man to track down.
EG: Like father, like son. [laughs] But really not a problem, I'm always happy to talk about the Fair and the Granters legacy. What would you like to know?

JS: I suppose first off, I'd be curious to know what you know about the original Fair?
EG: Well, I know everything - my father told me it all. I have access to all the memorabilia and files. I've devoured all the information I could on the event and other business matters.

JS: But what do you remember, you would have been - how old?
EG: I must have been in my teens at that point if we're coming up to the 50th anniversary.

JS: So as a teenager I imagine you would have seen a lot? I'm curious as to what you did at the Fair while your dad was working.
EG: I shadowed him a lot, I suppose. He wanted me to get the most out of the experience, it was a once in a lifetime event. So really whatever he knew, I knew, he made sure I was in the midst of it all.

JS: That's interesting. I hope you don't mind me saying, but I've been researching the event these last few months and I haven't managed to find one mention of you being there at all, or record of your attendance. I only heard of you when the rumours began about a potential anniversary event.
EG: Unfortunately I can't be held responsible for the documentation of the Fair, My. Scythe. There were many wonderful people there, all very busy with their own jobs. I suspect those in charge of keeping tabs of names were more focused on the paying public or official, higher profile guests than myself.

JS: Okay. I was hoping to ask you about the disruption at the Fair-
EG: Of course. I realise it's the most interesting part of it for many.

JS: Where were you when it happened? What do you remember?
EG: I couldn't say exactly, but I'm sure we were with the international delegates. There was a murmur of noise outside growing louder.

JS: What do you personally make of the rumours around the Stranger and Believers and the Fair?
EG: I find it interesting. It's a mighty fine thing to believe in. It's a fine thing to believe in anything. But the idea that the Stranger graced our own Fair, a being known for isolated appearances, well that's something. I suppose the Fair brought many people together who were grieving and seeking some relief or joy. On top of that they may have

found comfort and solace, assuming the rumours are indeed true. Who are we to say?

JS: Bit of a coincidence that the tagline is shaking hands with the stranger of tomorrow, though?
EG: Life is full of coincidences, Mr. Scythe.

JS: What about the Believers? What do you think about their tie to the Fair?
EG: Like I said, it's a wonder to believe in something. They seem to be, from what I've heard, overcoming darkness and living the most carefree of lives. They clung to the belief that death wasn't the end, and in turn - well, that's what they got. Again, as the rumours go. That's a mighty fine idea, isn't it? Death not being the end. Your life's greatest losses and still you have the opportunity to continue living, for who knows how long.

JS: Your dad seemed to share the same views, on the rare snippets I could find.
EG: I'm sure he did. Family traits.

JS: Family traits! You look so much like him in the old photos and videos, it's quite something.
EG: I do hear that a lot - we Granters have strong genetics.

JS: Clearly. So I was curious - the Fair was a success for the most part, the mystery around the Fair is something that your father at least partially had an interest in. Why did he clamp down so heavily on it? The legal trail of him doing so is quite brutal. And why run away for years after?
EG: Run away? I'm sure he travelled the world, not ran away. As for clamping down, he wanted to control the narrative around the Fair and keep it focused on the event itself.

JS: But surely the moment he saw it was causing more interest in the mystery - if it really was about the event - he'd do something?
EG: Well maybe he wanted people to care about something greater. It's a long time ago. I can't speak for him.

JS: There have been rumours that you might be working on something to celebrate the 50th anniversary in a few years - it's actually how I first came across you. Could you say anything about that?
EG: Yes, I'm thinking about it. The Echo seemed to run a speculative article drawing more attention than I had hoped at this stage. The location is tricky but if we can work something out I'm sure recapturing the spirit of that Fair would be utterly magical. There are no definites, but I'd like to think it's possible.

JS: That would be really great. I hope you do something to mark the anniversary - I'd do anything to experience the Fair in some form and I know many others are the same. I could only imagine how it felt to be there. A few final questions, if you don't mind. Jumping back a little

little bit, where were you in the year's following the Fair?
EG: I was... studying, I believe. Law. That sounds about right for the time. I travelled with my father too, saw the sights with him. Lots of big, exciting things. They blur into one another.

JS: But there is no record of your father travelling with anyone.
EG: Afraid that's not true!

JS: But all documentation shows he was travelling alone, and the files that were collected show no record of you even having a passport, let alone using it to the extent of your father.
EG: I'm sorry, Mr. Scythe, I don't know what you want me to say. It sounds as if this is about more than just the Fair and I think you've been looking into far too much for your own good. I know your previous role means you would have access to more files than most, but this feels like a real - and inaccurate - invasion of my family's privacy. I think it's best to end the conversation here. If I do manage to appropriately celebrate the Fair, perhaps our paths will cross there. Until then, I wish you well.

Bizarre

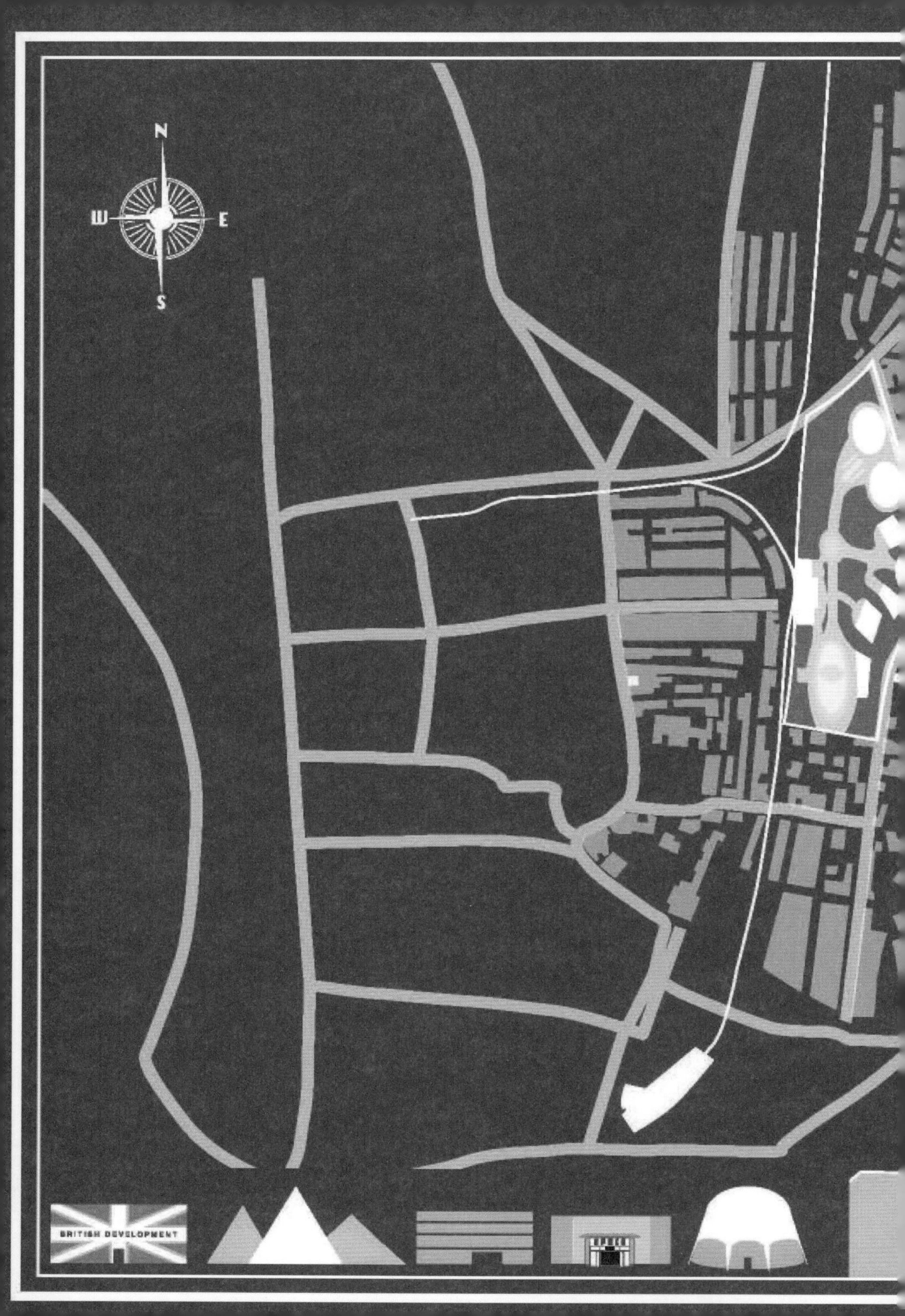
N
W
E
S
BRITISH DEVELOPMENT

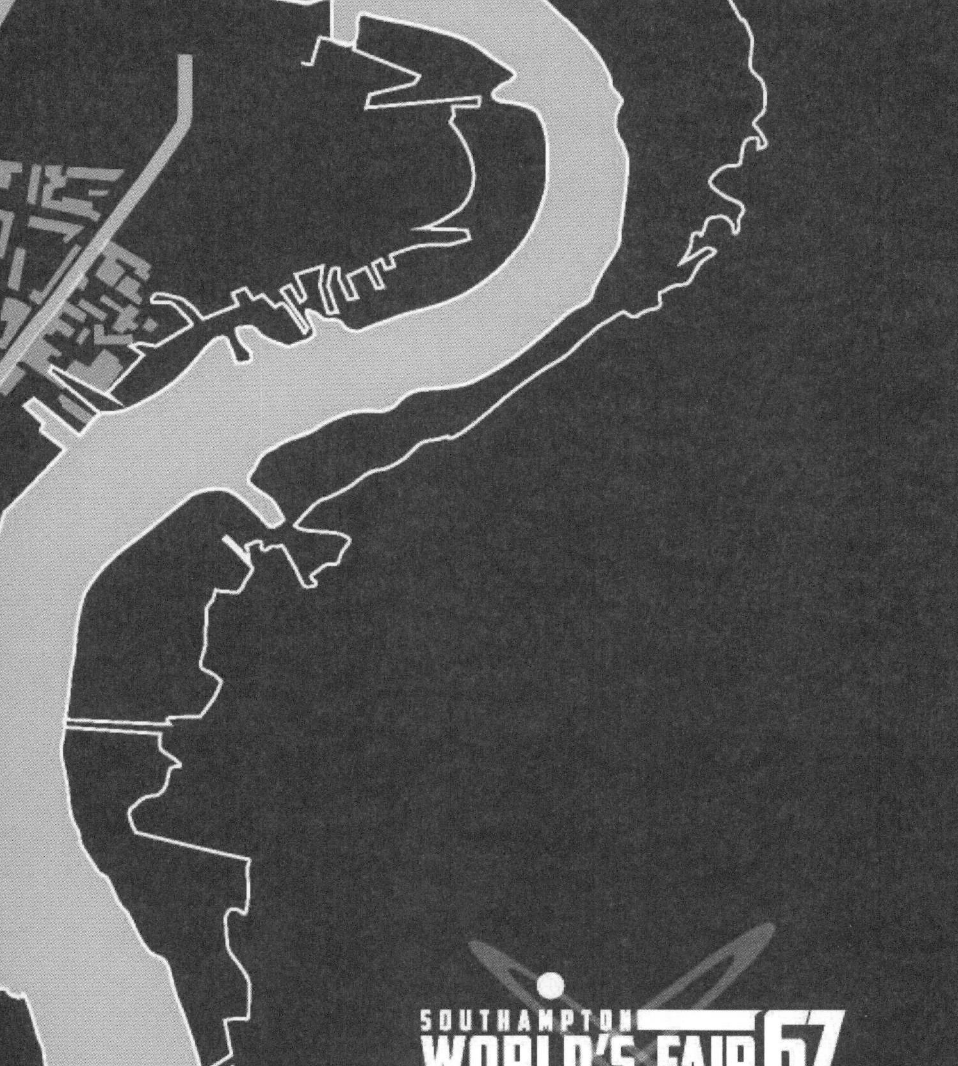
SOUTHAMPTON
WORLD'S FAIR 67
SHAKE HANDS WITH THE STRANGER OF TOMORROW

A MAP OF METROPOLITAN SOUTHAMPTON,
HAMPSHIRE FEATURING THE 1987 WORLD'S FAIR

0 10 20

ost infamous cases I have
;ards to the strange goings on
ton has to be that of The 1967
with much of the optimism of
; Fairs have sadly died out in
i'm sure there are many alive
:now what they are! Started in
ld's Fairs or EXPOs were a

Lilly,

I've attached a copy of the files we h
asked the team to do a little more dig
seen a discrepancy like this in decad
relevant.

World's Fair-wise, not my cup of tea.
I can gather from the team is that so

Had a look over the interviews – I wo
legends have been going around for
and for decades this has been ruled

If you don't mind me asking, why are
out what happened to James, not pie

George

Abandoned Southampton –

Helvetica 12

To: George Davies

Cc:

Bcc:

Subject: Re: World's Fair

George,

Maybe you came out the same people as you didn't choose to see what was right in front of you. You didn't believe.

Lilly

ranters. I suspect they'll largely be what you have already so apologies if that's the case. I've
on his son – as far as our records show Granters was the last in his line. Never married. Not
roves relevant to the disappearance of James, then the team can continue digging. But only if

sked around and we have the six dates and locations, and files that were already on file. The most
booked to play but no one's really heard of them.

lly cull them from the final report. Fantasists will only lead us further away from James. These
d even to our department are too far beyond the realm of the possible. We've seen many cases,
g not to pursue.

oking at the World's Fair anniversary tour? Because James was? You're losing focus. We're to find
here he left off. I hope you understand what I'm getting at and continue accordingly.

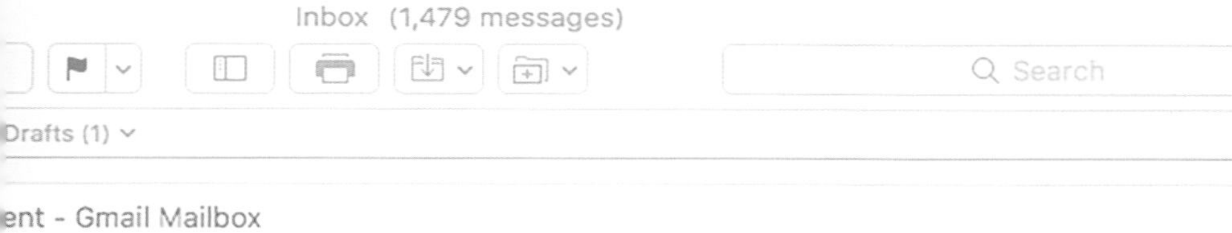

ies

Fair

ning

to sound like him. People have skirted around the topic but you need to hear it – over the months, you're becoming more and more l
ht in that we have been unable to solve what happened to James, but we all came out of the case the same people we went into it as
nd and don't lose yourself.

nt - Gmail Mailbox

ng

Fair

Davies

alling the interviews from the files. You can decide to ignore them upon the final report, but they're staying for th

u why these cases have been ruled as something not to pursue? Have you ever considered there might be a
ar? Ruling? Threats? There's too much out there for us – those who look into the *preternatural* to turn a blind ey
ook at the files, actually look at this. There's something there.

e going to take the case from me, I'd prefer you not dictate to me what I pursue – none of your team solved wh
nd until you do, I'm your best chance.

MARY

PAIN TRAUMA SADNESS

THE TRUE BELIEVERS

SURVIVE LOOK FOWARD ~~BRING BACK~~?

RING:
M MADAME DARLIN
OWN GRAVE?
NCER CURE
UCER RIDDLE

HSAYER
GAZINE

STRANGE H

New research — look into.

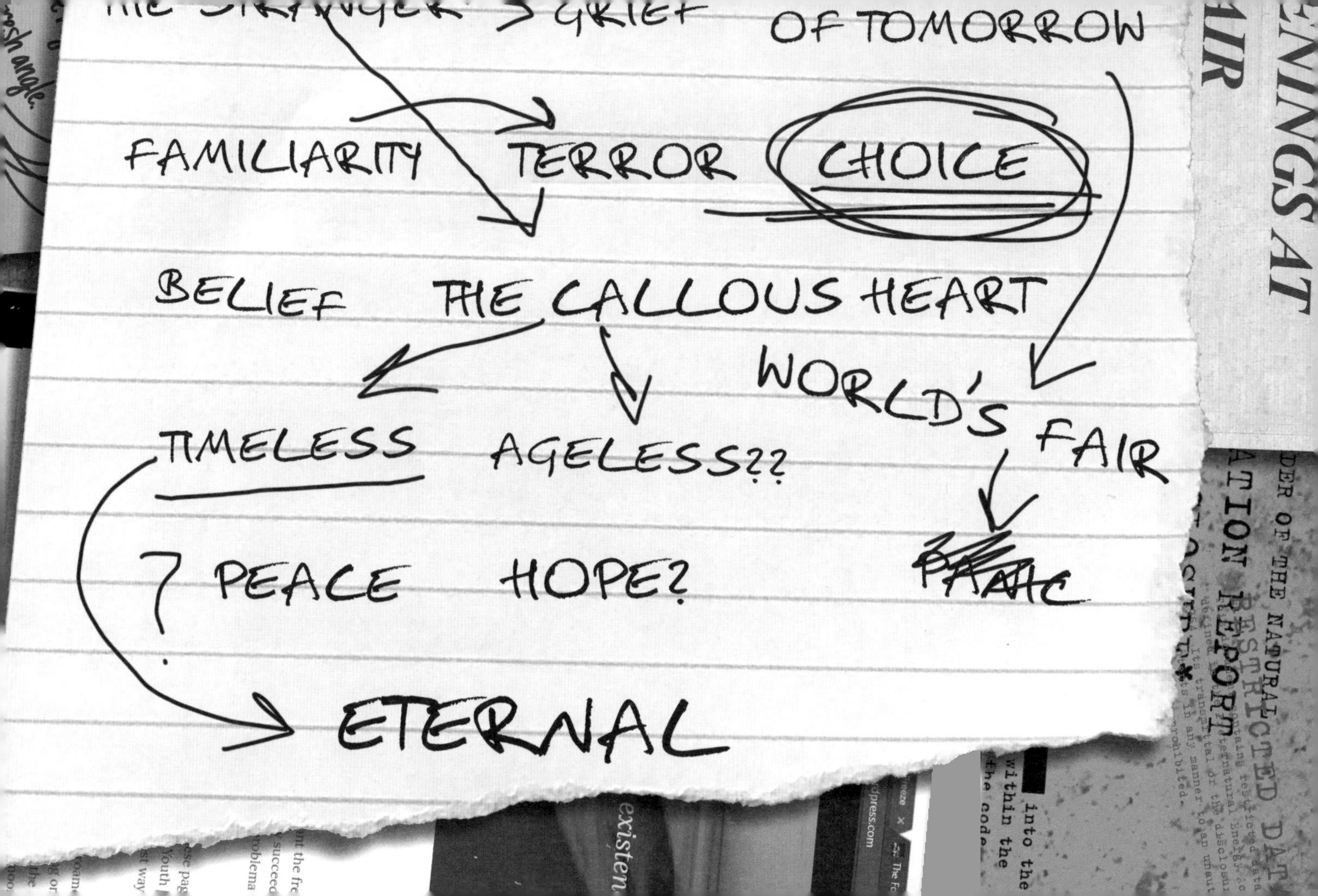
GRIEF
OF TOMORROW
FAMILIARITY
TERROR
CHOICE
BELIEF
THE CALLOUS HEART
WORLD'S FAIR
TIMELESS
AGELESS??
PEACE
HOPE?
ETERNAL
ENINGS AT
AIR
DER OF THE NATURAL
ATION REPORT
RESTRICTED DAT
into the
within the
existen

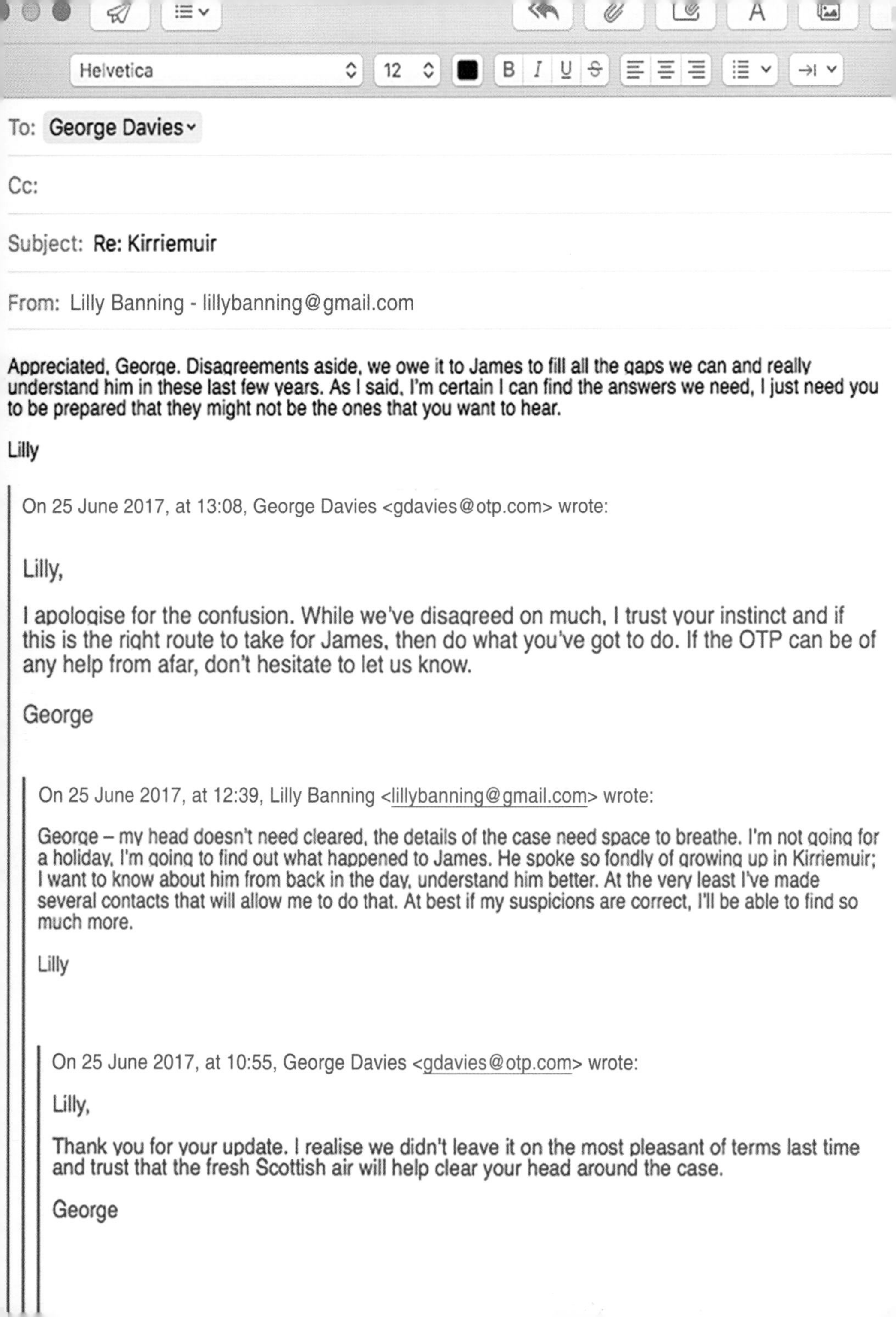
To: George Davies

Cc:

Subject: Re: Kirriemuir

From: Lilly Banning - lillybanning@gmail.com

Appreciated, George. Disagreements aside, we owe it to James to fill all the gaps we can and really understand him in these last few years. As I said, I'm certain I can find the answers we need, I just need you to be prepared that they might not be the ones that you want to hear.

Lilly

> On 25 June 2017, at 13:08, George Davies <gdavies@otp.com> wrote:
>
> Lilly,
>
> I apologise for the confusion. While we've disagreed on much, I trust your instinct and if this is the right route to take for James, then do what you've got to do. If the OTP can be of any help from afar, don't hesitate to let us know.
>
> George
>
>> On 25 June 2017, at 12:39, Lilly Banning <lillybanning@gmail.com> wrote:
>>
>> George – my head doesn't need cleared, the details of the case need space to breathe. I'm not going for a holiday, I'm going to find out what happened to James. He spoke so fondly of growing up in Kirriemuir; I want to know about him from back in the day, understand him better. At the very least I've made several contacts that will allow me to do that. At best if my suspicions are correct, I'll be able to find so much more.
>>
>> Lilly
>>
>>> On 25 June 2017, at 10:55, George Davies <gdavies@otp.com> wrote:
>>>
>>> Lilly,
>>>
>>> Thank you for your update. I realise we didn't leave it on the most pleasant of terms last time and trust that the fresh Scottish air will help clear your head around the case.
>>>
>>> George

2) Drafts (1)

Search

in Sent - Gmail Mailbox

e Davies

iemuir

Banning

GD

u for your update. I realise we didn't leave it on the most pleasant of terms last time and trust that the fresh Scottish air will
r your head around the case.

anning

uir

rge Davies

ge,

it's been quiet since our last email thread. I admit the frustration goes beyond our disagreement – I'm
myself becoming part of James' world far more than anticipated and that takes its toll. I know you are
he same page as me on where this is all pointing, but I can't stop following the thread, no matter
takes me.

ctively swept the piles of paper from the desk (metaphorically of course) and am starting a final new
I need to take a step back and see if this goes beyond the time we knew him, and also get some
from the rest of the case to see how it all fits together. This is just a note to let you know that should
d me I'll be up in Scotland for the next while.

at the answers are already there, we just need to reconcile our personal beliefs with what the files are
s, no matter how challenging that may be. My trip should put the final piece in this puzzle and give us
wers we need. I hope you are ready to hear them, even if they're not what you want.

ile is the only number to get me on. The signal might be temperamental but I assure you I'll be
able. I'm leaving tomorrow and will be heading to Edinburgh first before journeying on to Angus. I think
has reached its most critical point and I'm close to knowing who James has become these last few

shes

Spittal of Glenshee
Clova
Blair Atholl
Killiecrankie
Laurencekirk
Edzell
Stracathro
Kirkton of Glenisla
Pitlochry
Memus
Brechin
Kirriemuir
Montrose
Alyth
Forfar
Dunkeld
Blairgowrie
Coupar Angus
Arbroath
Monikie
Carnoustie
Scone
Crieff
Perth
1 h 54 min
80.0 miles
Bridge of Earn
St Andrews
Cupar
Falkland
M90
Kinross
Crail
Glenrothes
Leven
Anstruther
Alloa
Kirkcaldy
Dunfermline
Falkirk
North Berwick
Gullane
Linlithgow
East Linton
Dunbar
Ingliston
Haddington
Livingston
Dalkeith
Roslin
Carluke
West Linton
United Kingdom
FREE
English
welcometoscotland.com/app
Edinburgh In Your Pocket
Welcome to...
Edinburgh
2017/18
IVC
Irvine
Ayr
SOUTH

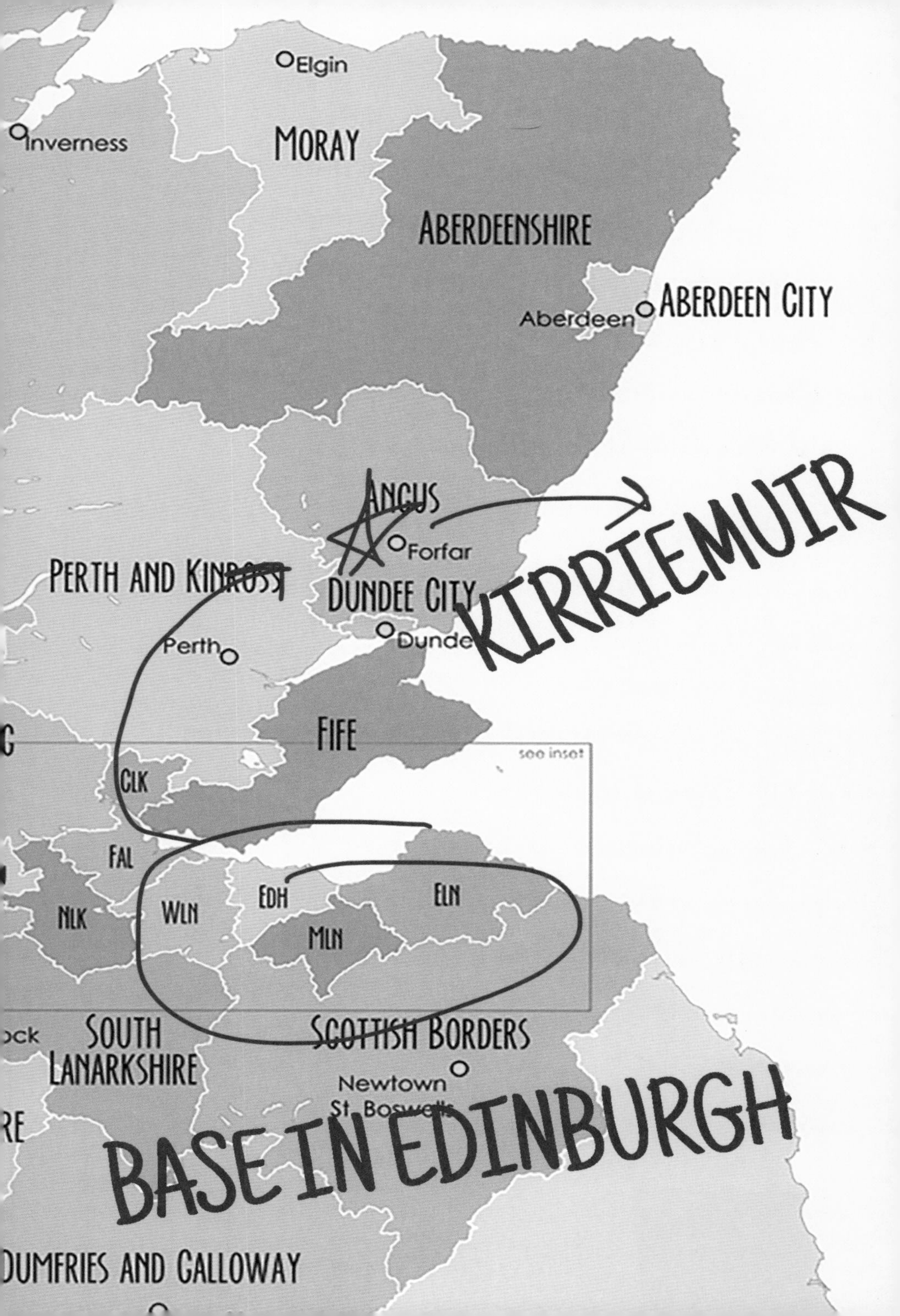

Elgin
Inverness
MORAY
ABERDEENSHIRE
Aberdeen
ABERDEEN CITY
ANGUS
Forfar
KIRRIEMUIR
PERTH AND KINROSS
DUNDEE CITY
Dunde
Perth
FIFE
see inset
CLK
FAL
NLK
WLN
EDH
ELN
MLN
SOUTH LANARKSHIRE
SCOTTISH BORDERS
Newtown St. Boswells
BASE IN EDINBURGH
DUMFRIES AND GALLOWAY

28 June 2017 – Kirriemuir

The Airlie Arms is nice. This whole town is surprisingly calming – very different to bustle of the city. Didn't know Bon Scott from AC/DC was born here and it was amusing to be greeted by his grinning statue. Would play the music but it seems too loud for the peace here. Not far from JM Barrie's birthplace too. Think I'll have a wander down between chats. I've passed at least one Pan statue so far, quite I can see why James liked it here.

People to chat to –

Police – No reports of him. Been out of trouble at least

~~Hotel staff~~ – no record of him – ~~using a different name~~?

~~Shopkeeper~~ – never heard of him; assistant doesn't recognise him

~~Barman~~ – can't remember him, probably served him

Café staff – Don't recall seeing him

→ Mrs. Jones says she remembers him. He came in for coffee regularly a little while and would sit on his laptop. Says 'a few years ago' when pressed said probably around 2014 as she remembered talking to him about the Commonwealth … to see rugby sever

~~School teachers~~ – Bar th

Suspicious of me looking

Word seems to be spreading that I'm asking around, it's raising suspicion. Need to rely on what's already set up and hope for the b One child referred to me as 'that nosy lady' on walk home.

Note: STOP ASKING AROUND!!!

Police. Hi Ms. Banning, thank you for waiting. We've checked the systems and barring his Missing Person report in 2015, we have no record of him. I don't know whether this news will be disappointing or not to you, but I hope you find him.

Shopkeeper. Hello. Oh, are you recording this? I'd rather you didn't. I'll answer any questions you have but I'd have to ask you don't record – it might pick up personal conversations of customers. [Audio end]

Café staff. We get so many people in here unless he's a regular I couldn't say. I'm sorry.
[Voice] I remember him. If it's the same person we're talking about.
L: When did you see him?
It would have been a few years ago. He came in for coffee and would sit for hours on end with his laptop or a book, and mostly read. I managed to prod him into talking on occasion. He was reading some great books. Frankenstein, revisiting Pan, couldn't say what else. He said he used to read all these books when he was younger. Became quite animated – nothing like talking about good books is there?
L: What year was this?
I couldn't be sure.
L: If you had to?
Oh, I think it might have been 2014? 15? When was the Commonwealth Games? I remember talking to him about that – I'd travelled down to see the Rugby Sevens. Great fun! My friends had no interest in that – more interested in the running and swimming – but he humoured me for a little while. So few new people come here without other people, so it's nice to chat to people. Do you perhaps have time for a coffee?
L: I'm afraid I don't. Maybe another time. Could I just get your name for my notes?
Of course. Mrs. Maggie Jones.

School: Hi Ms. Banning. We did wonder if you'd show up – had word of someone asking around! We can't give out any files on our students unless you are directly related or the student requires new copies of their results. We're not at liberty to give you contacts for any staff, current or previous. I'm sorry.

Valerie Young. Taught James in Primary, age 6-8. Northmuir Primary School

VY: James was a clever child. Very curious. Did his work, asked a lot of questions. Didn't struggle particularly with any subjects, just worked hard and was keen to learn.

LB: Were there any big moments you remember for him? Any life events while he was still in Kirriemuir?
VY: I wasn't his teacher at the time but when he was in High School his friend, Murray, was in an accident. Really knocked him for six according to the staff – you could talk to them. How do you explain grief and loss to someone that age? I don't know if he was still in Kirriemuir when his parents passed away; he was young in the grand scheme of life but I couldn't tell you if he went to University by then or not. He won the local spelling bee too with my class. Was very proud of himself.

LB: You're the only teacher I could trace down or who was willing to talk to me, so anything you know would be really helpful. Did he change much? After the loss of his friend?
VY: He seemed angry quite a lot, from what they said. It sounded more that he was mad people wouldn't leave him alone and kept trying to make him talk about it.

His grades didn't suffer. It seemed like he absorbed it, dealt with it himself, and came to school to just get school out the way, if that makes sense?

LB: Nothing in particular stood out at that time?
VY: As I said, I wasn't his teacher at the time so I couldn't tell you anything specific.

LB: What did you know of James after he left?
VY: I hadn't really thought about James until you got in touch. I had no idea he'd gone missing until you called – not many people did. They just assumed that when he left he'd gone down South again. You hear about the kids growing up and getting married but that's about it – too many to keep up with, and he was – with the greatest of respect to him – one of many children who came through the school.
LB: I understand. When was the last time you saw James?
VY: We're talking decades ago – I never did see him around after. The Andersons – Murray's parents – saw him quite frequently a few years ago. They said he was doing well, had never seemed happier. Though admittedly they only knew him in particularly dark times for the most part.

LB: When did they see James? Could you put me in touch with them?
VY: Couldn't tell you anything specific, sorry, but I'm sure I have their number

somewhere if that would be of use?

LB: That would be great, thank you. Is there anyone else you recommend I get in touch with while I'm here?

VY: I'm sure Susanne knows someone from the Scythe family, uncle, cousin removed or some sort – he won't talk to you on anything of interest, most likely, but he keeps the most meticulous collection of photos I've ever seen. If anyone in the town want to clear out their house, he'll offer to take the photos and keep an archive. Think he lost loads in a fire years ago and became quite protective of family legacies and such. I don't know if photos will be any use to you, but I'd say he's your best bet if so.

LB: At this point anything would be helpful, I think.

James' great grandparents

James as a young boy

Jeremy Scythe with his older cousin

INTERVIEW WITH FAMILY OF MURRAY ANDERSON
mother: Violet Anderson, father: Alan Anderson
29th June 2017

LB: So I just wanted to say thank you again for letting me come talk to you. I know this might be difficult, and if I overstep on any questions, please do let me know. I wanted to go back to the beginning and ask how Murray knew James? What was their friendship like?
VA: They were best friends. Murray always chimed on about James above everyone else. They didn't get up to anything wild from what I knew, just liked the same things – books, comics, shows. They ran aroun the outskirts of town a lot. Just very good friends.
AA: James was very nice too. Not to pick favourites over his friends but he was one of the quieter ones bu very nice. Mellowed Murray out a lot, Murray brought out a lot in him. I think, anyway.

LB: When the accident happened, did you see James much? How was he?
VA: We only saw him at the funeral properly. He was as everyone else was – sad. He was particularly quiet that day. His parents said he'd been quiet since the crash, and the school said that he was the one of all the boys who just seemed determined for him to get on with work.
AA: We did see him around at school occasionally when we'd come in to pick up our daughter Lily, or had a meeting with her teachers. Lily, good name. Frustration of her life was people spelling it with two Ls.

LB: Where is Lily now?
VA: Travelling the world at the moment. She makes a point of coming home at least twice a year and regularly stays in touch though. Living vicariously through her travels!

LB: So I've been told you spent some time with James in the last few years? Could you tell me about that?
AA: He came home at some point – seven, eight years ago now? He was renting a house by his old home. Looked for something quieter. We thought we saw him around a few times before we actually approached him to see how he was doing. Didn't want to go up to a stranger and freak them out.
VA: We invited him around for dinner and it became a bit more regular. He was here a couple of times that Lily was home too. That was nice. We'd talk about the older days, what he'd been doing, what we were reading, TV, the normal stuff. It was just nice to have someone round more regularly than twice a year, to be honest.

LB: And how was he? What did he say he'd been up to?
VA: He told us about Mary – the way he spoke about her, he really came alive. Such a shame what happened to her, and in such similar circumstance. He said he'd gone a little off the rails, nothing bad, but enough for his work to let him go. He decided the place he felt safest and happiest was in Kirriemuir. Said that getting old is overrated [laughs], and wanted to get away from the pressures of life for a while.

LB: But at some point he left and went back to Southampton – did you ever talk about that?
AA: A bit. In the last year or two of him being here he started talking about legends across the world. I think we'd been watching an Area 51 documentary – fascinating stuff. He gradually got more into that and started diving back through drawings and stuff from his childhood – he asked if we could keep a bunch of it as as he had to travel lightly. We've not touched it, but it reanimated him. He seemed to find purpose after wandering for so many years.
VA: He was happy here, but being happy and having a purpose is different isn't it? James wasn't cut out to stay here forever – he had so much out there to give, so many people interested in what he had to say.

Something ate him up inside after Mary and he needed to reconcile that. Without work, I guess he didn't have what he did at school to distract him from his grief and he had to confront it full on.

LB: Did he ever mention the Stranger?
VA: What stranger?

LB: The Stranger is... a being. A legend. He was quite into the research of it.
AA: We used to talk about it — Violet wasn't as much into the legends as I was. I found it quite uncomfortable really. I remember when he described it his eyes were lit up and I felt a sort of gut punch The dark figure — I feel like I saw him. But when you're grieving, you see death everywhere you look don't you? I've never felt pain like it, and so I've never, I guess in James' head at least, had cause to revisit my thoughts on it.

LB: But James..?
AA: James was so panicked after Mary. It was a horrific time, but he swears blind that he saw this dark figure. The way he tells it is he was terrified but gradually found more comfort from it. It visited his hor on the first night he was back after the crash and he pretty much passed out on the floor in fear. In tim he fully embraced it — fell into this wormhole of research.
VA: I think it's good to have something to cling to in dark times, especially if it brings you joy.

LB: You don't believe it?
VA: I can't say I heard James talk about it, but the only thing I was never sure of was his fascination with the otherworldly things. I like to keep my feet firmly in this world.

B: And you?

A: I have difficulty with it. What's the outcome if it's real? You feel better? I think that's a nice idea, but plenty things make you feel better and help you cope. James was certain there was more to it, but he was always sure things were bigger than they were. He left without saying goodbye. Should have seen it coming when he asked us to keep a bunch of his stuff, though. Just expected him to return.

LB: Would I be able to see what you've got from him?

VA: Sure. Alan, could you get it out the attic?

THIS BOOK BELONGS TO

JAMES

IF FOUND PLEASE RETURN TO

BRECHIN ROAD

READ AT YOUR OWN RISK!!!

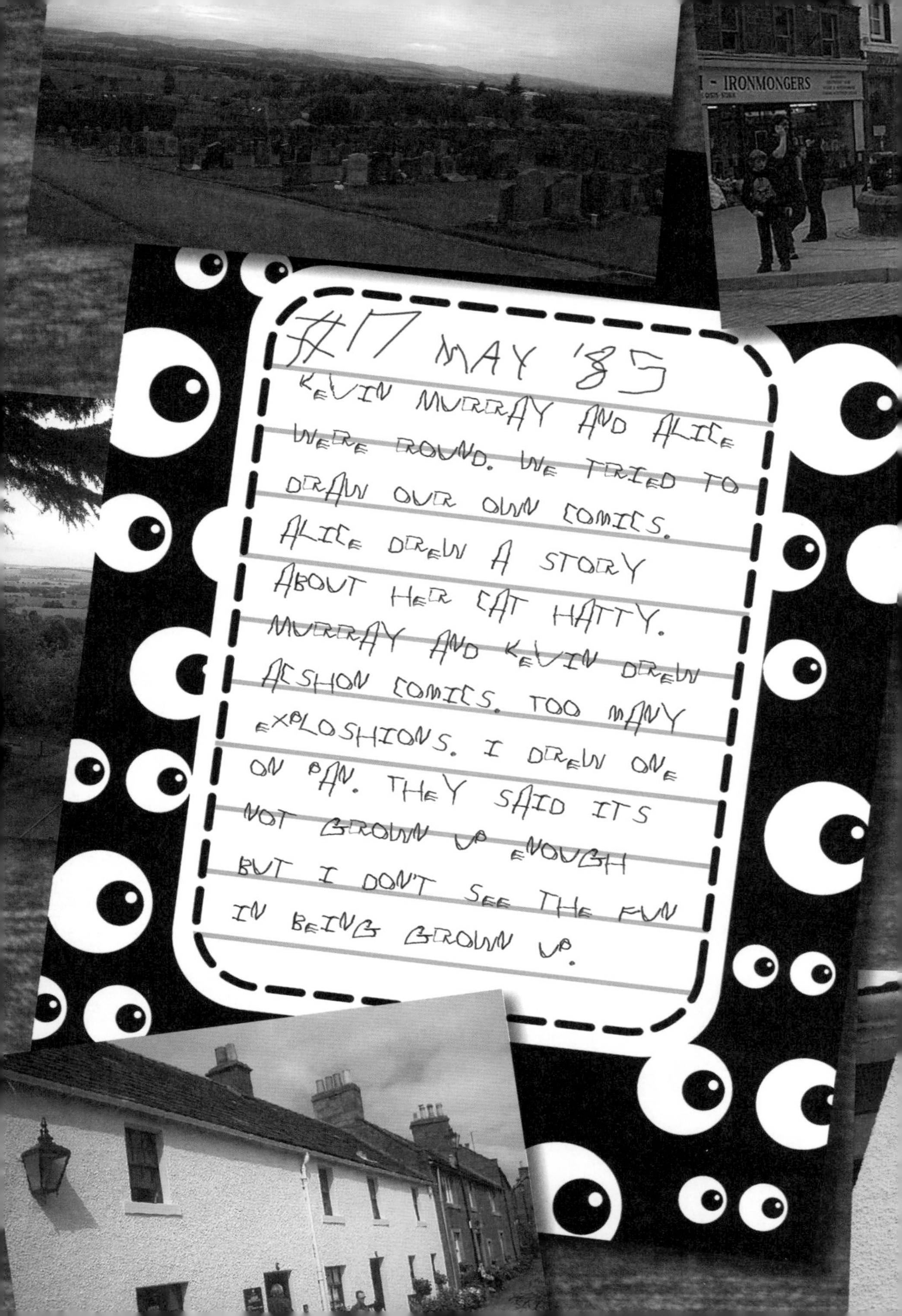
IRONMONGERS
17 MAY '85
KEVIN MURRAY AND ALICE
WERE ROUND. WE TRIED TO
DRAW OUR OWN COMICS.
ALICE DREW A STORY
ABOUT HER CAT HATTY.
MURRAY AND KEVIN DREW
ACSHON COMICS. TOO MANY
EXPLOSHIONS. I DREW ONE
ON PAN. THEY SAID ITS
NOT GROWN UP ENOUGH
BUT I DON'T SEE THE FUN
IN BEING GROWN UP.

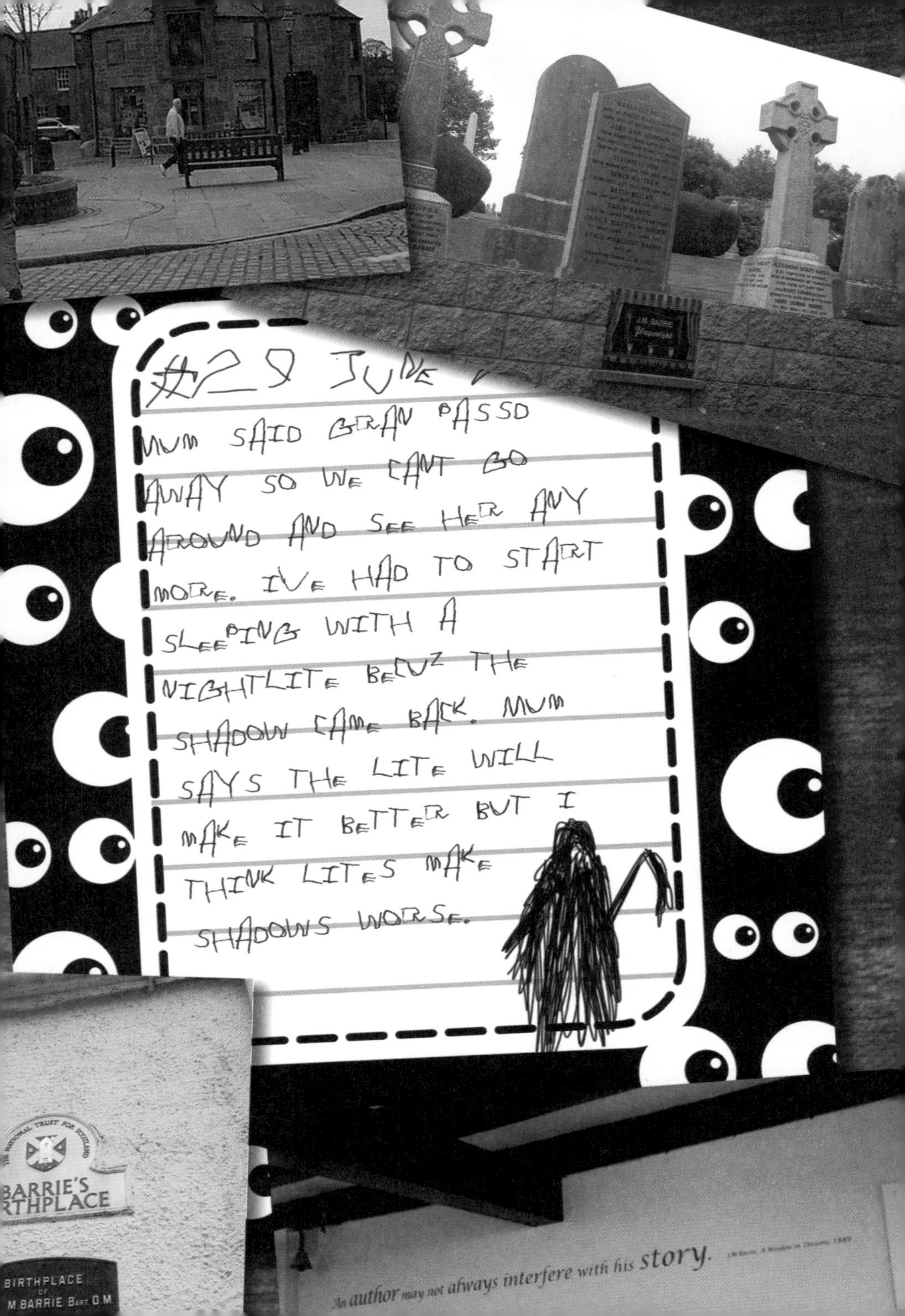
J.M. BARRIE
Playwright
#29 JUNE
MUM SAID GRAN PASSD
AWAY SO WE CANT GO
AROUND AND SEE HER ANY
MORE. IVE HAD TO START
SLEEPING WITH A
NIGHTLITE BECUZ THE
SHADOW CAME BACK. MUM
SAYS THE LITE WILL
MAKE IT BETTER BUT I
THINK LITES MAKE
SHADOWS WORSE.
THE NATIONAL TRUST FOR SCOTLAND
BARRIE'S
RTHPLACE
BIRTHPLACE
OF
J.M. BARRIE BART O.M.
An author may not always interfere with his story.

24.03.89

TODAY WAS PRETTY STANDARD. I CAN'T ESCAPE "I SHOU
BE SO LUCKY", EVERY TIME THE RADIO OR TV IS ON, I
BLARING. I'M SAVING TO GET SOME NEW ALBUMS —
HATE WOULD BE COOL BUT I KEEP BEING TOLD TO W
FEW MONTHS UNTIL IT'S OLDER AND CHEAPER. THE SH
DONT SEEM KEEN ON ORDERING ONE IN. SCHOOL I
THE SAME AS USUAL

15.05.89

THE SCHOOL KEEP BRINGING ME IN TO TALK AND SEE
NEED ANYTHING. IT'S AWKWARD. I JUST WANT TO GET ON
STUDYING AND GET THESE EXAMS OUT THE WAY. I DON'T
TO TALK TO THEM ANY MORE. THEY SMILE AT ME WEIRD
NOW.

17.05.89

DOES IT COUNT AS THE 17TH? OR EVENING OF THE 16TH? I
LATE EITHER WAY. I CAN'T SLEEP. I FEEL THIS WEIRD
TERROR SEIZING IN MY CHEST AND KEEP SEEING AN
OUTLINE AT THE WINDOW, BUT ON THIS FLOOR THAT'S
IMPOSSIBLE? I CAN'T BRING MYSELF TO LOOK OUTSI
(IF I DIE AND YOU'RE SOMEHOW READING THIS, LOOK
FOR THE PERSON WHO CAN SEE IN SECOND STOREY
WINDOWS!!!)

20.05.89

I DIDN'T DIE, OBVIOUSLY. I GOT A BIT LAZY ON UPDATING.
THAT NIGHT WAS ROUGH. I THINK I SOBBED IT ALL OUT. I
CAN'T REMEMBER FEELING SO BAD. I'LL REALLY MIS
HIM. IF HE SAW ME NOW HE'D PUNCH MY ARM AND CALL
ME A DORK. I KNOW IT'S STILL EARLY DAYS BUT PEOPL
ARE LETTING ME GET ON WITH THINGS RATHER THAN PUSHIN
ME TO TALK TO THEM. I PREFER IT THAT WAY.

01.06.89

EXAMS ARE TOO SOOOOOOO

Alan, Violet,

I just wanted to say sorry for leaving so abruptly. I appreciate you taking in my stuff while I returned to Southampton, though on arrival I'm not sure I'll be able to come home. Kirriemuir was the happiest time of my life and I'm glad that I was able to return in my darkest points and put myself back together — so this is really a thank you letter for helping me do that.

It's nice to revert to being young and ignoring the world's problems but I have some unsolved business that I need to tie up and can't put on hold any longer. I don't know how long it will take me, but I owe it to myself and Mary to follow it through. Alan, if you ever want to talk further about this, or Murray, you'll know where to find me.

Maybe I can't go back in time and undo it all, but I can try put a pi

...ke this time count.

A & V,

Do you still have that recipe for lasagne? In my clumsiness I think I've misplaced it and any of the recipes online pale in comparison.

A & V, November 2015

I think this might be my last letter, at least for a while. Don't worry, nothing bad. In fact, incredibly good. I think I'm on the brink of solving it all. The worlds I've seen, the possibilities I've witnessed – I think I'm getting a second shot to make everything right. I just need to believe in it enough, and need them to believe in me. This month I'm going to make them take notice of me, show that I really do believe. I can overcome.

Where that will take me, or when I'll be back, I don't know, but trust me, this is it.

J

CLASSIFIED

To: George Davies

Cc:

Subject: The Last Days of James Scythe

From: Lilly Banning <lillybanning@gmail.com>

Dear George,

It's with a heavy heart I'm writing to you. I've been quiet the last while as I battled on what to do next following my trip to Scotland. When you asked me to return to the team, I knew I could get to the bottom of what happened to James. As you said, everyone else came out of the case the same person they went into it as. I feel I will not be the same again, but I also have uncovered the answers everyone before me struggled to find by suspending my perceived notions of reality and following where James led me.

This all comes down to your belief.

I have attached all the documents I could unearth, and all relevant correspondence. I thought – we all thought – he was smothered in grief. It's true, he never did recover from the loss of Mary. He was agitated, delusional, frantic when we knew him – he was becoming a different person in front of us. Grief was part of that, but I can't bring myself to say that it was all that there was. I know we've all scoffed at his ramblings, we've all raised an eyebrow at his obsessions, but…

It's difficult to find the words. I've found myself following the threads of his last few weeks, months, years, and slowly being pulled into these worlds. What happened to James Scythe? Part of me worries you, just like the others, wanted a quick fix answer to make everyone feel better – he upped and left to start a new life, no need to worry! He's fine!

To me, he became the mystery he dedicated his life to solving. James Scythe is in the pages of his own notes, the lines of his own stories. I believe that somewhere he is fine, and he has found peace, but that's not in death, nor a fresh start elsewhere. He is here, somewhere, and will show himself when he's happy and truly ready to face the world again.

I know what it sounds like, but I'm asking you to trust me. Look at the files, *really* look at them. You'll see that while his last few years were tinged with grief, he

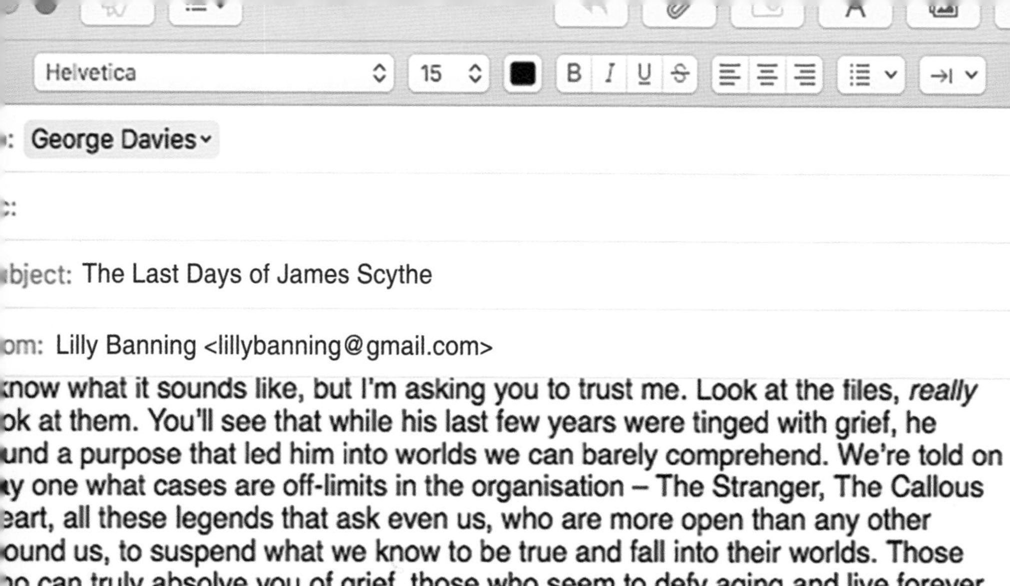
Helvetica 15 B I U S

: George Davies

::

ıbject: The Last Days of James Scythe

om: Lilly Banning <lillybanning@gmail.com>

‹now what it sounds like, but I'm asking you to trust me. Look at the files, *really*
ok at them. You'll see that while his last few years were tinged with grief, he
und a purpose that led him into worlds we can barely comprehend. We're told on
ay one what cases are off-limits in the organisation – The Stranger, The Callous
eart, all these legends that ask even us, who are more open than any other
ound us, to suspend what we know to be true and fall into their worlds. Those
ho can truly absolve you of grief, those who seem to defy aging and live forever,
e purest of light and dark. Have you ever asked yourself why? Who told us never
look into these worlds? I say it's a greater challenge. To discover and follow
ese threads you need to go above and beyond in search of something greater,
u've got to overcome your own hardships and believe in something greater.

can't say I'm fully there yet, and I daresay you're nowhere closer to this than
hen we began. But it's there – let yourself fall into these worlds. Believe.

can't say where James is, but I'm certain one day he'll return. The implications of
s return, however, I don't know I can fully process. I'm not there yet. I can only
ispend my reality so far, but it's far enough to see what's right in front of me. If I
rn out to be right, I don't know that I can be around to see it. I only hope that if I
n right then it was worth it for James, that he got the second chance at life he
as after.

n signing out of this email before you have the chance to reply, and you'll be hit
th my eternal out of office when you do. I'm starting afresh. I need to get away
fore I slip any further out of this world and into theirs. Please don't try find me. I'll
tucked up somewhere with a good book, you can count on that much.

till believe in James Scythe. I hope you do too.

ly
lillybanning / lillybanning.wordpress.com

The James Scy

Case Files

[CLOS

Notes

INCONCLUSIVE:

Lead investigator Lilly Banning provided inconclusive evidence

SEPT 2017

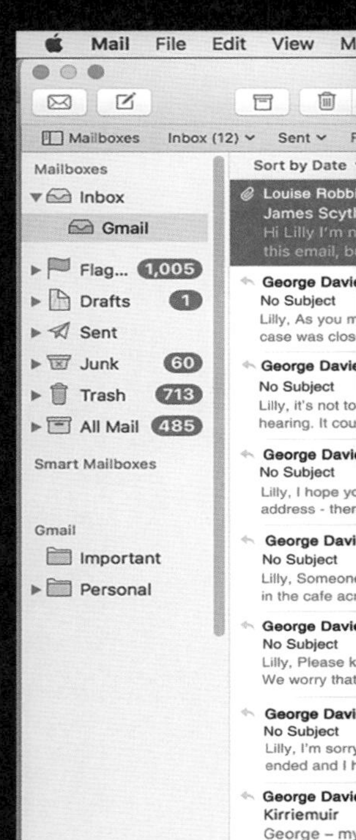
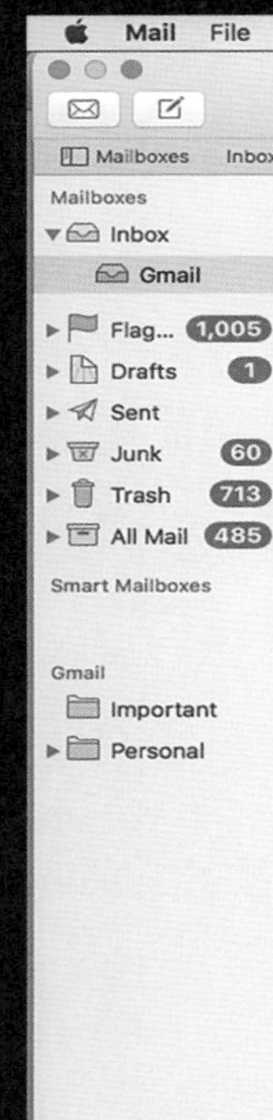
Mail
File
Edit
View
Mailboxes
Inbox (12)
Sent
Mailboxes
Inbox
Gmail
Flag...
1,005
Drafts
1
Sent
Junk
60
Trash
713
All Mail
485
Smart Mailboxes
Gmail
Important
Personal
Sort by Date
No Subject
No Subject
No Subject
No Subject
No Subject
No Subject
Kirriemuir

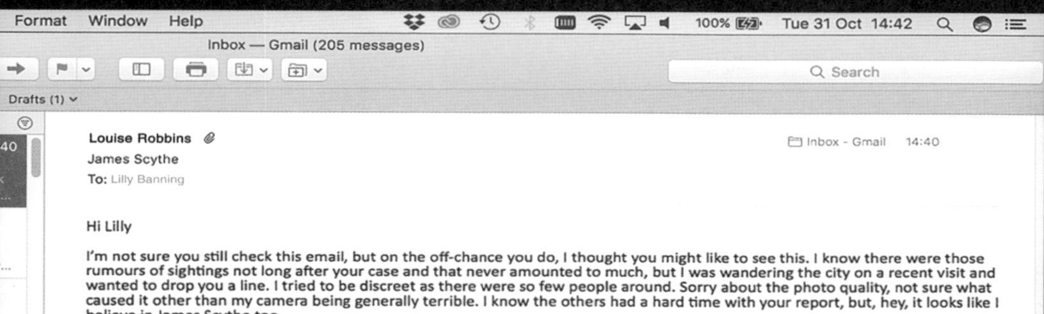

Hi Lilly

I'm not sure you still check this email, but on the off-chance you do, I thought you might like to see this. I know there were those rumours of sightings not long after your case and that never amounted to much, but I was wandering the city on a recent visit and wanted to drop you a line. I tried to be discreet as there were so few people around. Sorry about the photo quality, not sure what caused it other than my camera being generally terrible. I know the others had a hard time with your report, but, hey, it looks like I believe in James Scythe too.

If you do check this, I hope you're doing well, wherever you are.

Don't be a stranger.

Lou

Photo credits:

+ Denotes licensed under CC BY 2.0
++ Denotes licensed under CC BY-SA 2.5
+++ Denotes licensed under CC BY 3.0
++++ Denotes licensed under CC BY-SA 4.0
* Denotes edited by 404 Ink

P38: "Statue on Titanic Engineers' Memorial, Southampton" by Marek.69 talk. https://commons.wikimedia.org/wiki/File:Statue_on_Titanic_Engineers%27_Memorial,_Southampton.jpg +
P38: "The Woolhouse, Southampton, June 2014 (3)" by Richard Nevell. https://commons.wikimedia.org/wiki/File:The_Woolhouse,_Southampton,_June_2014_(3).jpg +
P38: "Southampton medevial walls and Catchcold Tower" by Michael Coppins. https://commons.wikimedia.org/wiki/File:Southampton_medevial_walls_and_Catchcold_Tower.jpg ++++
P38: "Tudor Merchants Hall" by Jhsteel. https://commons.wikimedia.org/wiki/File:Tudor_Merchants_Hall.jpg +++
P38: "Sir Isaac Watts, Watts Park, Southampton – geograph.org.uk – 1727766" by Christine Matthews. https://commons.wikimedia.org/wiki/File:Sir_Isaac_Watts,_Watts_Park,_Southampton_-_geograph.org.uk_-_1727766.jpg +
P39: "Southampton west gate" by Sun2Shine. https://commons.wikimedia.org/wiki/File:Southampton_west_gate.jpg ++++
P39: "Tudor House, Southampton – geograph.org.uk – 1733014" by Peter Trimming. https://commons.wikimedia.org/wiki/File:Tudor_House,_Southampton_-_geograph.org.uk_-_1733014.jpg +
P41: "Kowloon Motor Bus buses for export at Southampton Docks 2" by Arriva436. https://commons.wikimedia.org/wiki/File:Kowloon_Motor_Bus_buses_for_export_at_Southampton_Docks_2.JPG +++
P46: "A very beautiful old lady II" by Pedro Ribeiro Simoes. https://www.flickr.com/photos/pedrosimoes7/443738371 *+
P60: "Ruins of Holy Rood Church, High Street, Southampton, Hampshire - geograph.org.uk - 893770" by Oast House Archive. https://commons.wikimedia.org/wiki/File:Ruins_of_Holy_Rood_Church,_High_Street,_Southampton,_Hampshire_-_geograph.org.uk_-_893770.jpg *+
P60: "Southampton – Bargate.JPG" by Christophe.Finot. https://commons.wikimedia.org/wiki/File:Southampton_-_Bargate.JPG *++
P82: "SOOTHSAYER" by aka Tman. https://www.flickr.com/photos/rundwolf/4271916049 *+
P103: "HighStreetGaietycirca1930.jpg" by User:Hethurs. https://commons.wikimedia.org/wiki/File:HighStreetGaietycirca1930.jpg *+++
P104: "Westerham Carnival" by Andy Parrett.geograph.org.uk/p/4349652 *+
P132: "Scotland Administrative Map 2009" by XrysD. https://commons.wikimedia.org/wiki/File:Scotland_Administrative_Map_2009.png *+++
P144: "Barrie's Birthplace, Kirriemuir" by Richard Slessor. http://www.geograph.org.uk/photo/105807 +
P144: "Kirriemuir Town Centre" by Mike Pennington. http://www.geograph.org.uk/photo/1233345 *+